BOOK FOUR
IN THE
LOVE & FATE
SERIES
BY
JEANETTE ROSE & ALEXIS RUNE

ROSE & STAR PUBLISHING

To All Readers Who Wished For A Light To Shine Into Their Darkness.

---

[1] *It should be noted Melinoë is driven insane by the things she experiences as the Goddess of Nightmares, at no point should she be considered an accurate representation of humans who experience either of these disorders.*

Chapter One
Melinoë

FUCKING HELIOS.[2] . Fucking clingy ass glowing weirdo. I curse him with every step I take toward his building. I curse his glowing skin, vibrant personality, and washboard abs. But most of all, I curse the way my skin anticipates his touch. I hate the way my inner madness purrs for him when I look into his eyes. I never feel more on the edge of falling into the pit of my mind than when I'm with him, not even when I'm in the Underworld. Yet, even though I toe that treacherous line, I also never feel more sane than when he is near.

The clarity of him…

The birds chirp happily. They have no fucking clue that I'm on my way to ask the most incessantly annoying person I know for a favor. Gods know what it will cost me. He had actually called me his girlfriend during our last encounter.

Ugh. Tying myself to anyone is barbaric. But a Titan? A Titan who has the sun shining out of his ass? Gross. I've always been more comfortable in the shadows, and when I'm around Helios, there are no shadows where I can retreat.

Fucking sunboy.

My stomach does a strange kind of somersault at the sight of his apartment building. I stop walking and growl down at it, "Do that again, and I'll enjoy driving a knife into you."

The flutter in my stomach doesn't cease, but a man coming toward me on the street gasps and backs away, his face pulled into an expression of gut-wrenching fear. I look behind me, trying to find the cause before realizing it is me. I grin at him and wave. The dude takes another step back and trips, falling onto his ass. His eyes are wide and glistening in a way I've only seen from those entering the bowels of Tartarus.

I used to laugh then. Their fear made me feel powerful. It made my madness purr in a way that made it difficult to resist, and I often didn't. I blink at him, feeling the pull of his fear, the madness calling to me oh so sweetly. The laughter bubbled up in my chest, but then…

"Help me, Mel!"

Her soft voice paws at me, the dulcet tones of my best friend locked in my head. Is my mind any safer than where she really is?

I look away from the dude who is now crying. He is chanting something about not hurting him, but I can barely hear it. Helios's apartment practically shines in the distance, and I move toward it as if called.

Albert, his doorman, sits at the desk, sorting through some mail. I salute him on my way past, and he gives me a curt nod in return. I hit the button repeatedly for the elevator. Persephone's voice is gone now, but my eagerness to see Helios is amping up. I tell myself it's only because I need him to check on my best friend. Of course, it's nothing more. It's not because I want to lick him head to toe and taste his sunshine on my tongue.

The elevator opens directly into the penthouse, and his scent hits me, pleasure plunging straight between my legs. Not only does Helios radiate sunshine, but he smells like it, too. Then, there is a faint scent of coconut mixed in that makes me want to lean into him and inhale deeply.

I see Helios immediately. He is lounging on his balcony, holding one of those foldable mirrors, no doubt to feed his vanity, along with topping up his stupid tan.

"Hello, hellcat," he purrs, not even turning to look at me, but I can practically see the smirk on his stupid, beautiful face.

"Sunboy," I growl.

Helios turns his head, his golden eyes piercing into the blackness of my tortured soul. He crooks his finger. I bristle at his unspoken command but struggle to stop my feet from moving toward him. My body needs to move in some way, so I placate it by crossing my arms over my chest. "I need you to do something."

Helios's lips pull into a smirk, and he crooks his finger

again, a picture of ease.

Motherfucker.

I lift my chin, quirking a brow. "It's time-sensitive."

He doesn't move; he just keeps me locked there with his penetrating stare. My skin feels like it's on fire, and I have the urge to rip it off just so I can offer it to him.

I growl, low and dangerous, but slowly walk toward him. Within ten steps, I can feel his heat. Within eleven steps, I am close enough, and he reaches for me. Before I register what he's about to do, I am on his lap, straddling him.

He digs his fingers into my hips and smirks up at me. "What do you need, Melinoë?" he asks. The way he says my name sounds so sinful that a shock of awareness tightens my belly.

I clench my fists. The effort it's taking to keep my face hard and my expression unaffected feels like I've just completed a five-mile sprint.

"Persephone has been taken."

Helios's smug smile drops, and I feel his whole body tensing beneath me. He sits up a little, his fingers pressing into my hips, holding me there. "Demeter?"

I nod once. "I think so. Hades is completely freaking out and asking for ridiculous things, so… I need you to go to Olympus."

Helios tilts his head, his eyes searching mine, seeing something in my expression that's making him pause. "What is he asking for?"

My whole body goes tense with the knowledge of the danger we all will face. "Cross-realm dreamwalking."

Dreamwalking is never something I recommend, though in my younger days, when I didn't care what side of the madness threshold I walked on, I dreamwalked all the time. Sometimes, I would just pop in and observe, hiding in the shadows, watching the depraved and wild things the unconscious mind conjured up in others. Sometimes, I was more active, and that was definitely the more dangerous of the two.

Dreamwalking by myself is inherently dangerous. It is very easy to just… lose myself into the oblivion of a stranger's mind, intertwining my madness with their lucidity until my voice is as prevalent in their brain as their own. But dreamwalking with another is a whole other ball game. It should only be attempted with a person who has a strong mind and will and only with someone like me who is experienced at dreamwalking. Cross-realm dreamwalking increases the risk of losing yourself tenfold and requires two more often than not. One to access the dream, fucking asshole Morpheus, and someone to pull from the dream, me.

"He is being an idiot." Helios's eyes continue their exploration of my face.

I can practically see him cataloging every curve, dip, and micro-expression, and I remind myself to keep my face neutral.

"He's beside himself. Persephone's link with him and the Underworld has been severed and—"

Helios pulls me against his chest, cradling my head in the crook of his neck. He nuzzles me, and I feel him inhale deeply. Fucking weirdo.

"Uh… what are you doing?" I ask, my hands braced awkwardly against his chest.

"I'll leave in five," he murmurs into my hair, stroking my back. "As for what I'm doing… I am cuddling my girlfriend." I can hear his stupid panty-dropping smile, and it makes my fucking blood boil.

I shove away from him, growling, "I am not your girlfriend. Get away from me, you weird, clingy fuck."

Helios chuckles and pulls me back into his chest.

Gods, has he always been this strong? Am I actually even fighting him?

"I get ten minutes of this in exchange for going to Olympus," he says into my hair.

I blink. "You're extorting me for affection? Really? And as payment for a favor to help someone who is also one of your best friends?"

He inhales deeply again, his nose in my hair. "Looks like it."

"Helios, Persephone is—"

"Persephone is with her mother, who will not harm her," Helios states, confident and commanding.

I sigh heavily, giving in. "Let's just get this over with," I grumble.

I can feel the pleasure radiating from him, the mushy dickbag. My body remains tense, not used to prolonged affection from anyone. The longest I've held someone was Persephone when Hades was being a moron, and that was different. She's my best friend, and I actually like her. This is unbearable.

"I hate this," I mutter after what feels like an eternity of him holding me in this stupid wrestler restraint move.

I feel him kiss my head softly. "I know," he replies, and I can feel the smile in his voice. His heartbeat thrums happily beneath me, beating with the smugness he seems to feel.

"Gods, is it over yet?" I ask, wrinkling my nose in distaste.

Helios lifts his arm, checking his watch. "Still got… nine minutes and thirty-five seconds."

I groan loudly, muttering in discontent. Helios pulls my resisting body closer and nuzzles into me. I hate to admit it, but within a few minutes, my body does start to relax into his, but I am sure it is just the warmth of the sun against my back. Soon, the steady beat of his heart is kind of soothing or… whatever.

"I'll find her, hellcat. We'll get her back." Gods, how does he do that with his voice? How does he make it trail over my skin like the most filthy of promises?

I relax more into him, but my body becomes more aware. Every inch of skin that he touches tingles, and I fight to keep from purring like a kitten for him.

Helios lifts some strands of my black hair, twirling it around his finger. "I know you're worried…"

"Yes, and you're causing me bodily distress by insisting on this death embrace," I growl. Although the way my body has melted into him, every one of my words is a contradiction.

He snickers, obviously hearing the lie. The tips of his fingers glide across my back. His touch is light but sure, like an artist painting on a canvas. "Is that what I'm doing?"

I try to lock my spine, but my effort is futile, and I can't hold back the shiver. "Yes," I reply, trying to push as much hatred into that one syllable as I can.

"You must be in… so much distress." I can hear the way he tries to hold back his stupid fucking smile. Smug bastard.

"I hate you," I growl.

Helios moves his hand, gently pressing his fingers underneath my chin, lifting my head so my gaze locks with his. Warmth floods my stomach, and I'm certain it's his pelvic sorcery Titan shit that he's using to trick me.

"Kiss me," he practically growls, his gaze drifting to my lips.

I force my upper lip into a snarled curl. "I'm about to knock you out."

Helios's lips pull into a bright, almost dazzling smile. Fuck, when did I start looking at his lips?

"So much foreplay for just a kiss."

I narrow my eyes, leaning in and hovering my mouth over his. "Time's up, sunboy," I say, snapping my teeth at his lips before moving off him, needing to put as much space between us as possible. Helios slaps my ass, and I gasp. The sharp sting heats my cheek, but it's not the ache there that concerns me. It's the one between my legs that is consuming all my attention.

I whirl on him, snarling, "Do that again, and I'll enjoy feeding that hand to Cerberus."

Helios stands and stalks toward me, as graceful as a lion and with a smirk plastered on that maddeningly beautiful face. He draws his hand back and swings it, planting another hard smack on my ass cheek.

The moan slips past my lips before I can quell it, and Helios's eyes darken at the sound.

"Cerberus is going to be thrilled with his new toy from Aunt Mellie," I growl, pretending the groan of pleasure was nothing but his imagination, but we both know it happened.

Helios backs me into the wall, bracing one of his hands against it, caging me in. I crane my neck to look up to him, my nostrils flaring in anger. He swoops his head down, slamming his lips to mine, kissing me with the fire of a thousand suns. My whole body warms with need, but I fight him. I push at his chest and growl until… until his tongue sweeps over mine, and I get that taste of him. Fuck.

Get it together, Mel! I pull back, slapping him hard across the face.

Helios slowly turns his face back to mine, his expression feral, his eyes almost completely black. He moans, licking the corner of his lip. I pant, looking him over, and I'm not sure what happens, but suddenly we're kissing again. This time, instead of shoving at his chest, I lock my fingers into his hair. Our teeth clash in our need to be closer, both of us working to own the other, to taste more, to be more. Helios's fingers tangle in my hair, and he yanks hard, pulling some of the strands free. I snarl against his lips, but the pain pushes me on, only deepening my need for him.

I grasp his mostly open shirt and clutch at it, swapping our positions and shoving him hard against the wall. He groans at the impact, his hands moving to my tits, my hips, my ass, his touch searing me.

"Come get it, hellcat," he growls into my mouth.

"Mellie."

I curse and pull back, panting. "Go. Now."

Helios pants, looking me over hungrily. "You owe me when I get back," he says, his voice a deep rumble.

I move in closer again, grabbing his face roughly and

narrowing my eyes. "I owe you nothing, sunboy."

Helios grabs my ass hard, his fingers digging into the flesh almost painfully. I bite back the moan.

"Oh, you definitely do, and I'll make you purr for me."

I groan and pull his face to mine, devouring his mouth. I bite his lip so hard it bleeds before pulling back. "Go."

Helios smirks at me, the sight of his bloody lip sending a shock of desire to my pussy. He winks, and in a flash of sunlight, he's gone.

Chapter Two

Helios

O LYMPUS. For all its manicured greenery, blooming flowers, and shining white marble, it is the opposite of welcoming. The winding path to the palace where the king and queen reside is marked with the abodes of various gods and goddesses.

How many times have I climbed this path since the war? Since siding with Zeus against my own king? Yet, I've never felt the need to skip up the path until today. My steps have never felt so light, and it's all because of a little mismatched-eyed hellcat. My body is still humming from that little interaction. I lick my lip, disappointed that it had already healed. Fuck. I love how violent she is. After I find Persephone, I'm going to enjoy fighting with her. My skin glows in anticipation. I want her madness. I want her sanity. I want her violence. I want her to purr when I make her happy. I want her.

The sight of a bright chiton drags me from my musings, and I blink for a moment, stunned. Persephone's hair is pulled back so tightly it distorts the features of her face, and her chiton flows around her body, disguising her form.

Okay, what the fuck?

"Petal!" I call out to her, pasting a smile on my face as I close the distance.

She keeps walking down the path away from me, idly touching the flowers. Did she not hear me?

I close the distance, grabbing her hand. "Petal?"

She gasps and jumps away from me. A shiver of unease shoots down my spine. Persephone doesn't react like that. She reminds me of a fawn who sees a hunter in the distance.

"Persephone?" I ask, looking into her eyes. They're vacant.

It's not in the cute way that Mellie's eyes go vacant when she's thinking of ways to murder me. It's more like the… no-lights-on-inside kind of way. She blinks at me, and there's no recognition in her eyes.

"Yes?" she asks, her voice grating to my ears. Not because it's rough or unusual. It's soft and gentle.

Not Persephone.

"Persephone, we really must get back," a nymph calls, intruding on the moment.

Her head turns toward the nymph. "Right, let's go," she says and hurries off, leaving me standing there, stunned. Whoever that was, it was not Persephone. I need to tell Mellie.

I flash back to my penthouse, looking around. "Hellcat?"

Even after the disconcerting encounter with Persephone, my body is primed for an attack from Melinoë. I have zero shame in admitting that I'm excited for her to launch herself at me. Hopefully, she has her nails sharpened into claws and plans to slash them across my face.

Fuck, she's so unhinged. And so fucking hot. My cock is already twitching to life. I frown when there's no attack from a deranged goddess. I duck into the rooms, finding them all empty. Little hellcat, she wants to play? We'll play. I find the note she left on the inside of the freezer door. No doubt she put it in the place I would be least likely to look.

Just text me, loser.

I smirk and start making a kale smoothie since I am in the kitchen before pulling out my phone to text my errant nightmare goddess.

HELIOS

Back from Olympus.

MELLIE

That's nice. What's the report?

I pour my smoothie into a glass and take a long sip, taking my time before responding. I can practically hear her grinding with annoyance.

HELIOS

If you want to know you'll have to get back to my place.

It's a different kind of addiction playing with Mellie like this. I imagine it's like what mortals feel when their adrenaline is surging. Mortals go skydiving. I tease a feral goddess until she physically attacks me.

MELLIE

BRB, just going to report to the king of the dead that you're withholding information regarding his queen.

I smirk and finish off my smoothie before washing the glass and putting it on the drying rack. She must feel backed into the corner if she's relying on her connection to Hades in order to force me to comply. But I have another card to play.

HELIOS

Feel free to report to your adopted dad that you failed in his task. I'm sure that won't have him thinking about dreamwalking again.

There's a long pause, enough for me to strip down to my briefs and head out to my lounger.

MELLIE

If you touch me, you're putting your life in my hands. And I'm feeling stabby.

HELIOS

Fuck you're sexy, hurry up.

I relax back on the lounger, smirking.[3]

Chapter Three
Melinoë

THE ELEVATOR ASCENDS AND I IMPA-
TIENTLY PACE. How am I here twice in one
day? Fucking Helios. The small ding as every
floor passes seems to set me more on edge, but I need my
game face on. I'm here for information only. No kissing.
No touching. No thinking about anything but Persephone.
The doors open, and my eyes immediately meet Helios's
gaze. He takes a slow drink from the large white plastic
bottle, the ever-present smirk plastered on his face.

I enter the room just far enough that the elevator door
can close behind me, leaving as much space as possible between Helios and me.

"And where did you go?" Helios asks, tilting his head.

"The information," I practically growl my words, allowing myself to fall into the frustration I feel when I'm
around him, letting it fuel me.

Helios's smile widens.

Oh, you want to play, sunboy? Let's play. I saunter across
his living room, stopping before the cabinet against the
wall. The peach-colored wood fits perfectly with the nude
and beige tones of the apartment. The shelves are tastefully
cluttered with expensive-looking ornaments and trinkets.

I tilt my head as I look over a particularly precious-look-
ing one, carefully gliding my finger over the shiny glaze
and the tiny blue triangles that stand out against the ghost-
ly white background. I lift my head, meeting Helios's gaze
again as I slowly nudge it toward the edge of the shelf.

Helios doesn't move, but a thrill of excitement sparks
within me at the slight tension of his shoulders. He nar-

rows his eyes, acknowledging my challenge.

I lift an eyebrow, waiting another moment before nudging it again. The sound of it smashing against the hardwood floor fills the room, and sharp pieces of broken pottery fly everywhere.

"Oops…" My lips curl into a thrilled smile, waiting for him to react.

Helios's jaw tightens, but he still doesn't move, his body wracked with tension.

Oh, sunboy, how I love playing with you.

I take a couple of steps, choosing the next victim. Helios winces with every crunch of his broken pot beneath my biker boots. I curl my finger around the neck of a small vase, moving it once again to the edge. The scraping sound of the ceramic grating against the wood makes the hair at my nape stand.

I wait for Helios to make his move, giving him another chance, but to my surprise, his jaw ticks slightly, and he takes another drink from his bottle before turning and giving me his back.

How fucking dare he! For a split second, I lose all sanity, and my anger plunges me into madness. I wrap my fingers around the vase and throw it at him hard.

Helios anticipates my move, and with a near-blinding flash of light, the vase shatters mid-air, sending pottery everywhere. He keeps his back to me, not even bothering to look at me, and I throw another vase, then another, then another. Each one, Helios blasts to smithereens before they hit him.

My hand comes up empty when I reach for another one. I glance at the cabinet, seeing that it's now empty. I snarl and turn, stalking toward the elevator, my blood boiling and my hands shaking from the insanity that I'm trying desperately to quell.

"You're leaving without the information you need, hellcat?" he purrs.

I stop, my hand hovering in front of the elevator button. "Did you see her?" I don't even recognize my voice, so distorted by my fury.

I wait for Helios's reply, but it doesn't come. I turn to face him again to find him looking at me. He beckons me, pointing at the floor in front of him. "Here. Now. No games."

I clench my fists, weighing my options. Helios is still the better of two evils. Fuck. I walk over to him, muttering about how Hades and Persephone owe me fucking big time.

I stop in front of him, and his hands land on my hips, pulling me to stand between his legs. I glare at him, but his thumbs stroke maddening circles against my bare waist, and it's making me feel funny. As usual, in his presence, I find myself still walking the tightrope between sanity and insanity, but because I can see him, smell him, feel him, it's like there is glass just below the rope. Even if I fell in the direction of madness, I would simply be looking down at it.

"I saw her," Helios finally says, keeping his gaze locked on mine. "But only for a second."

"But you saw her?"

Helios pulls me closer. "Yes, but something was off." His brows furrow, and he looks away, thinking. "A nymph rushed her away."

I blink. "A nymph? Gross. Okay. How did she look?"

Helios pauses for another moment. "Almost… happy."

"Well fuck me, Helios. How am I supposed to tell Hades that? And that doesn't even make any sense."

Helios keeps doing that infuriating movement with his thumbs. I can tell it's to comfort him as much as to infuriate me. "There's more." He sighs. "But I'm not sure you can tell Hades this part."

I lift my eyebrows. "What are you talking about?"

Helios meets my gaze. "I don't think she knew who I was."

I blink, then blink again, my mind racing with every conceivable reason that could be. It could be anything from amnesia to the lighting to… memory wiping.

"Fuck fuck fuck fuck fuck." I pull away, pacing. "What the shit am I supposed to do with that information? Are you telling me you think they took her memories from the past… two and a half years?"

Helios watches me carefully. I can feel his eyes on me, but he makes no move to touch me. His first smart move.

"I'm not telling you anything except that she is fine, physically at least. And she's being allowed outside of her mother's villa, though, with a chaperone, it seems."

I continue my string of curses. "Is it possible she just didn't see you properly?" I ask, continuing to pace.

"I mean… it's not impossible. She's also never seen me in my Olympian clothes."

He's delusional, and so am I, but I'll hold on to every scrap of hope in order to not tell Hades what I think I'm going to have to tell him.

I nod. "What do I tell him?"

"You could tell him that—"

"Fuck, fucking dickwad Morpheus is already preparing to dreamwalk him. Fucking arrogant asshole motherfucker," I interrupt.

"Tell him that her mother hasn't harmed her and that she's being allowed outside of the villa," Helios says louder this time, but I continue pacing. I swear I'm about to burn a trail on his hardwood floor. I continue muttering to myself about cross-realm dreamwalking, about the danger, and about how much of a fucking dickhead Morpheus is.

Helios steps in front of me, grabbing my face hard and forcing me to look at him. "And when you do dreamwalk with him, I'm going to be there," he says matter-of-factly.

I blink up at him. "Are you insane?"

"Honestly? Maybe a little. But I will be there because I know it will endanger you as much as Hades."

I snarl, yanking away from him. "So you think adding another consciousness into the mix will be helpful?" Mellie scoffs. "Apparently, you're a dumbass, too. You'll get on swimmingly with Morphie."

"I love when you're mean to me. I thought you might want someone who crosses realms into Olympus present." He smirks, his skin glowing a bit more. "Plus, I'm good for your concentration."

"Arrogant, pretentious prick," I growl, clenching my fists.

"Fuck, insult me more," he practically moans.

I slap him across the face, trying not to notice the effect his moan had on me. Helios grabs me and pulls me against him. He sweeps his arm over the kitchen island, clearing it before lifting me to sit on it. He slams his lips to mine, and I'm immediately lost in them. The sound of the kitchen utensils and mugs hitting the floor barely registers over my moan.

Helios bites my lip, and I taste copper as blood weeps from the wound, the pain making me even more feral for him. My hands roamed over his smooth, golden skin. Fuck, he is always so warm, so soft, so perfect for sinking my nails into… or my teeth.

My hands roam over his bare chest, exploring every inch, every dip and curve of his abs. His skin beneath my fingertips makes me long to melt into him, needing to feel his heat sinking into my bones.

Helios plunges his fingers into my hair and yanks, angling my head to the side. His lips trail searing kisses down my neck, and I dig my nails into his shoulder harder, making him groan. He sinks his teeth into my neck, and I arch my body against him, my moan nearly a gasp. His hands slide along my back, raking his nails over my shirt, the fabric tearing beneath his touch. He rips away the remaining scraps of my shirt, my shorts following. I kick them away and push at his briefs, desperate to have him naked. Helios growls and pushes me back. Spreading my thighs achingly wide, he plunges into me. His cock stretches me almost painfully, sending waves of pleasure through my body.

"Fuck, slap me, hellcat." His groan is guttural, and I know he is just as feral for me as I am for him.

"I fucking hate you," I growl, slapping him hard across the face.

Helios's answering moan is the reward I didn't know I needed, and he slams into me harder, grabbing my face roughly and hovering his lips over mine. "You hate the way I fuck you, Melinoë?"

I drag my nails down his chest, leaving angry red lines. "I hate everything about you. Your touch. Your kiss. Your cock," I snarl.

Helios slams his lips to mine, biting my lip again, re-opening the already healing wound. He pulls back, his lips bright gold, covered in my blood. Fuck me. That's the hottest thing I've ever seen.

"The only thing you hate about me is the way I make that tight pussy purr," Helios growls, licking my blood from his bottom lip.

I feel the blood from my lip slide down my chin, and I yank Helios's head to the side. I wipe the blood on his cheek before whispering in his ear, my voice almost sweet, "My pussy hates you the most."

Helios yanks my head back, slamming into my cunt harder and faster. My arousal slides down my thighs as he runs his thumb through the last drop of blood on my lip and drags it along my throat. I throw my head back, baring my neck to him. "You're repulsive to me."

Helios pinches my nipple, sending pain tripping through me. "Good," he growls.

I move my hands to the edge of the counter, trying to stabilize myself.

"You going to come, kitty?" Helios asks, his lips against my jaw, his sinful fingers twisting my nipple deliciously.

His words send a wave of fury through me. I slide one of my hands between my legs, circling my clit and taking control of my own pleasure, not wanting to give Helios any part of it.

Helios snarls, yanking my hand away and slapping my clit. I arch but growl at him, quickly moving my other hand between my legs and stroking my clit once. Helios grabs my hand. But that one touch was enough, and he's too fucking late. I arch, throwing my head back as I come hard, my pussy clamping around his cock. Helios shouts, following me over the edge, digging his fingers into my hips.

I pant, immediately pushing him away and moving off the counter. My legs feel like jelly, but I will myself to stand up straight. "That… was the last time," I growl, pulling my ruined shirt back on and looking for my shorts.

Helios licks his lips slowly, brushing his fingers over the drying blood on his cheek. "That's what you said last time, hellcat. But here's the problem…" He backs me up against the kitchen island again. "You know you can't get this anywhere else, and you can't get enough. That's why you keep coming back," he says, caging me in.

I poke him in the chest hard, punctuating each word. "The. Last. Fucking. Time."

Helios leans in, nuzzling my jaw like a fucking lion with his lioness. "What are you going to tell Hades?"

I smack him away, feeling trapped. "That isn't your concern."

Helios growls, kissing me deeply, and I can't help but kiss him back. Fuck, I need to get out of here.

"You know that it's stupid not to include me.

"No. What is stupid is what just happened," I hiss.

Helios tunnels his fingers into my hair again, tilting my head up. "Let's go to the Underworld then."

"You can't go without an invitation," I growl.

"I'll talk to Hades, and you can start thinking of an explanation as to why you didn't bring me in the first place." Helios brushes his nose over mine.

I hiss again. "That's easy. It's because I despise you."

"Afraid for them to know how I make you purr?"

"You make my skin crawl," I snarl at him, baring my teeth.

Helios slips his hand into my panties, thrusting two fingers inside me. "Crawling to soak my cock, maybe."

I try to hold back my moan, but it's impossible. "I'm… thinking of someone else."

"Oh? Do they know that you're full of my cum right now?" Helios slowly thrusts his fingers inside me.

I growl, shoving him back. Helios smirks and brings his

fingers to his lips, sucking them clean. I hiss and flip him the bird before turning and leaving his apartment.[4]

---

4 The Queen & The King Chapters 5 - 9

Chapter Four

Helios

I FOLLOW AFTER MELINOË AS SHE LEAVES THE UNDERWORLD, going to her apartment. I pull out the key I had made and unlock the door, walking in like I own the place.

She snarls at me over her shoulder but doesn't stop pacing. She's worn a steady line in the carpet. No doubt this is where she constantly paces when trying to figure something out. I head to the bar to make a drink. I hum softly to myself as I make a tequila sunrise. She keeps muttering to herself. I swirl my drink before tossing it back, preparing myself for the fight with my kitten.

I step into her path, wrapping my arms around her, snapping her from the spiral. "Give it a second. Your mind is still reeling."

She looks up at me, her eyes still vibrating with her dance with insanity. I expect her to hit me. I'm braced for it and a little aroused by it, if I'm being completely honest with myself. Instead, she kisses me suddenly. It's a silent cry for help, a sign of how close that darkness is to swallowing her whole.

Just don't leave me behind.

I cup her head, keeping her against me. There's desperation in her kiss, a call begging me to stop the descent. I answer. The sun is the center of this universe, propelling planets around it. I can pull Melinoë back from the brink, catching her in my gravitational pull. I lift her into my arms and carry her into the bedroom, careful not to break the kiss. Laying down with her, I stroke her hair, keeping her body pressed to mine. Her heart is beating so rapidly that I can feel it against my chest.

This is nice. Melinoë is cuddled into my chest, letting me comfort her for the first time, but it ends as soon as it begins.

She shoves away from me and stands up. "Leave."

I watch as she starts pacing, but I am decidedly not leaving.

"Why?" I ask, trying to predict her next move. With Melinoë, I could never guess. She could kiss me or stab me in the hand. Either way, I am in.

I stand up and walk toward her, cautiously closing the distance. She looks up at me, her eyes flickering with an emotion I rarely see from her—vulnerability.

"I don't want you here," she says, but her eyes say don't leave me.

"I'm not going anywhere," I whisper, cupping her face. She has such a small, delicate face, with soft skin like porcelain. Everything about her is deceptive, meant to make you think she is gentle and meek. Then she opens her mouth.

"Go. Now," she hisses, shoving at my chest. I don't move at all. She's better with weapons than raw strength. "I fucking hate you! Leave!" she screams, shoving me again harder. My feet remain firmly planted. "Fight me! Hate me! Leave me!"

I don't move. I only stare.

Her dual-colored eyes are shaking, showing her lucidity. This isn't her dance with insanity. This is sane Melinoë. It's something much deeper. She grasps my shirt desperately, her eyes showing what she can't say. Don't leave me.

I scan her eyes. "I'm falling for you."

Melinoë pales, all the fury and emotion draining from her face. She releases me and steps back. I stand still. I probably shouldn't have admitted that. Whatever. I felt it. So, I said it.

I reach out and wrap my arm around her back, pulling her back into me. When she doesn't resist, I smile, kissing her softly.

She pulls back. "You should… go check on Persephone."

I kiss her again. "Probably."

Instead of leaving to check on her, I walk Melinoë back toward the bed.

She whispers shakily, "Helios…"

I press my lips to hers, drinking in all the taste of her emotions. I lift her into my arms, and she doesn't struggle. Instead, she digs her fingers into my hair. We fall onto the bed in a tangle of limbs, and I take my time kissing and licking down her body until I've got my face between her legs. I worship her with my tongue, even as her fingers tighten in my hair. I sink three fingers into her and bite her clit, loving the taste of her blood as I sink my teeth in deep.

She screams so loud as she comes that my eardrums burst from the pitch. My healing kicks in almost immediately, and I lap at her pussy one last time, groaning at her taste. I keep an eye on her face as she comes down, kissing her hip before shifting back up her body. I press against her and rock my hips between her splayed thighs, kissing her deeply.

She breaks the kiss and glares up at me as she levels off. "You need to go."

I kiss her hard. "I know."

I roll off her and sit up, glancing at her over my shoulder. "I'll be back, though. Will you be here?"

She shrugs.

"Kiss me," I growl at her.

"No," she growls back at me.

My eyes narrow on her. "Now."

Melinoë's eyes darken, leaning in and pressing her lips against mine tightly.

I sink my teeth into her lip. She's so fucking addictive. "I'll find her. I promise."

She pulls back. "Whatever."[5]

Chapter Five
Helios

OLYMPUS. TWICE IN TWO DAYS. That's more than I've spent there in the last four thousand years. Even when Titans controlled the ruling seat of the gods, I hated it here. It's fake. Every smile, every platitude, every long look hides a thousand truths and a thousand aching wounds. Fuck, unlike Melinoë. She has no idea how easy she is to read most of the time. The truth lies in her pale eye and the lie in the dark one.

Damn, how much longer am I going to have to spend in Olympus before I can go back to sparring with Melinoë? Preferably with weapons and plenty of violence. I never thought I would be into those two things, but with Melinoë, everything and anything is on the table. She wants to stab me? Done. She wants to torture me? Even better. Who really gives a fuck as long as it ends with me buried inside her?

I looked around and grimaced. Gods, I hated this place. Not that I ever fit in with this crowd. There is no clearer divide between the divine than Titan and Olympian. It is like wearing a tattoo across my forehead that says enemy. You would think I would have at least earned some goodwill after willingly renouncing my former ties. I'd even gone so far as to give up some of my abilities to one of Zeus's thousand whelps as a part of my "rehabilitation". Selene and Eos had to do the same.

It's one of the beautiful little perks of being on the losing side of a god war. That, and the distrustful looks of Olympians as I walk past, the way they shuffle to the other side of the cobbled pathway so as not to cross my path. I do my best to ignore it all and continue to stroll forward, but I release a breath when I see Persephone hovering over a patch of flowers. She's dressed in another demure gown, her hair pulled back in a painful bun.

It should be the perfect painted picture, but every single part of it is wrong. It's in the way she holds herself and the way her gown is a little baggier than the one I saw her in previously. She's focused on some flower, touching the petals wistfully, but for a moment, she looks so… broken. The worst part, though, is that she looks confused as if she doesn't understand why. My stupid heart aches at the sight.

"Persephone?" I call, unable to see that shattered look on the friend I've known for over two years. I can't let this happen to Persephone. Her fucking bitch of a mother has already taken too much from her—her memories, her style, her confidence. I would try to give her a bit of herself back if I could.

She lifts her head and looks at me. Her eyes are dull, even though her smile is kind. "Yes?"

Persephone stands, brushing some of the lingering dirt off her hands. I barely cover a sneer at the sight. Persephone may be the Goddess of Spring, and she loves flowers, but this image of her kneeling in the dirt is still wrong. She can wave her hand and have the flowers thriving, yet she's struggling to fertilize them? No doubt, Demeter insisted on teaching her humility. Fuck humility, and fuck Demeter with a cactus.

"I didn't get a chance to introduce myself the other day, but I'm Helios," I offer, looking for any spark of recognition in her eyes. I had hoped that I had imagined it the last time I was in Olympus, that she did know who I was. But her stare is blank. Nothing.

I remember the first time we met in the mortal world. She was arguing with a florist about the way the flowers were displayed. Especially because the florist was a man and told her that if she had such strong opinions, she should open her own store and stop bothering him. The verbal takedown I witnessed from her that day was glorious. I doubt that florist ever truly recovered from it. I insisted we needed to be friends immediately, and part of my sunny disposition is being completely charming.

"Oh, lovely to meet you, Helios. I'm…" She pauses. "Well, I suppose you already know my name."

I chuckle. There is a little bit of the sass I remember in her tone. It's the same one that turned that florist into mulch. I hear it again when she laughs softly with me, a little more of the Persephone I remember there.

"How do you know my name exactly?" she asks, a bit of suspicion leaking into her tone.

I suppose it is odd to have a Titan approach you randomly as you're gardening. Persephone has always been clever. That hasn't changed.

"Well, you're all the talk on Olympus," I replied smoothly.

It is not technically a lie. Persephone is the talk of every Greek Pantheon realm, from the Underworld to Olympus. It's not an enviable position, especially not for me.

"Oh, I am?"

I shift to lean against a tree, nodding. "Well, of course, your mother finally letting you out has drawn a lot of attention."

Her eyes flicker with hurt, and I step closer. "What?"

Her guard goes back up, and she shutters the emotion behind her eyes. "I think I want to move these here." She points to a bed of bright yellow flowers, then to a bare patch of soil. "And these here." She points to some red ones and then to the other patch.

I don't know much about flowers, and I wonder what kind of flowers I should get for Melinoë. Hmm, maybe one of those deadly ones. I don't think Persephone would point me to some belladonna or hemlock. I don't know if people really grow those in their gardens anymore, but they should.

I open my palm, forming a miniature sun, directing it onto the flowers she was working on. "I could help. Sunshine for the flowers?"

Her eyes narrow slightly on me, and she waves her hand over the white ones, making them grow instantly to their full size.

There you are, petal.

"Persephone! Lunch!" Demeter calls, and her eyes dart in panic back to the house. I doubt she notices that the white flowers sag a little in response.

"Coming, Mother!" she calls back, looking at me. Every trace of the Persephone I remember is gone, sucked out of her by just the sound of her mother's voice. I squeeze her arm, silently assuring her.

We're still here, petal. We'll still be here when you come back.[6]

Chapter Six
Melinoë

HADES' EMBRACE STILL CLINGS TO ME LIKE A CLOAK OF HOPELESSNESS AND DESPERATION. In all our centuries together, he has never hugged me, never even tried to.

I can still taste his fear on my tongue. There's the surface fear, the fear you would expect. He wonders if Persephone is being harmed, that she will never regain what she has lost. But it's the last one that coats my skin like warm jasmine-scented oil. The fear of being alone, of losing his mate. The fear that he has not only lost the love of his life but also himself. And the most potent, most delicious, was the fear of the darkness. He thinks I can't sense it, that my inner madness isn't purring for it, but I know it's there. It will consume him if he doesn't get it under control.

Hades believes he cannot be manipulated, but he is wrong. In my many years of knowing him, I have devised the perfect algorithm for when to bring up certain things. I have used the knowledge to my advantage many times. Or at least, I used to. Now, he is too volatile, and I'm acutely aware that should he unleash even a tendril of that darkness in my presence, I may plummet to a depth of insanity from which there is no coming back.

The center of the living room is my favorite place to pace, so much so that I have worn myself a pacing track. My mind whirls with thoughts, various voices chiming in, both helpful and not.

The previous dream was a disaster, as expected. It almost collapsed in on all of us, which would have left us trapped in the fucking ether world forever. The dream did not feel stable when we entered it. Fucking Morpheus.

"Yes, my king. Of course, my king. Let me kiss your asshole, my king."

Fucking asshole. I snarl at the thought of him, and the voices become louder in my head, some of them practically roaring to be heard over the rabble. I'm vaguely aware of the sound of my own muttering as I try to formulate a plan, but they're so loud that my head is pounding.

"So close, Melinoë… How easy it would be to just—"

My head snaps up when I hear a cupboard door close. In a flash, I'm there, lunging at the large body who dared intrude upon my space. I pin the brute to the wall, my eyes still hazed from my thoughts, the voices only slightly quieter.

"Hey, baby." His voice is like sun-warmed silk, and my eyes snap clear as it caresses my eardrums. Even the voices within recede to barely a whisper.

A snarl rips from my throat as my brain catches up to my immediate reaction to him. I need to nip that in the fucking bud. Why can't my body find him as repellant as my mind does? I press my forearm harder against his chest, and he responds with a low growl, his fingers slithering into my hair like the venomous cobra he is, biding his time until he can imbed those weird mushy fangs into my neck.

"Hi," he says again, his skin doing that incessant glowy thing.

"Why are you here?" I snarl. I can tell by how his pupils swallow his dazzling blue eyes that he can see my wildness.

"Here, hellcat? In my penthouse?" He tilts his head, the ever-present, infuriating smirk tugging at his lips.

My whole body tenses, and I pull my gaze from his, looking around the room. My eyes burn a little from the brightness of the room. The terracotta and peach tones are all the evidence I need to prove him right, and I curse my fucking powers, mind, and body for bringing me here, for being comforted in a place like this. In his fucking place.

Helios roughly tugs my hair, forcing my attention back to him. I curl my lip, glaring at the stupidly beautiful face staring back at me.

His smirk deepens. "Give it to me, baby."

That damn pet name again. Oh, I'm going to rip out his fucking tongue.

"Give me all of your madness." His eyes sparkle, and I can't help but stare into them for a moment longer than I want to, searching for something, though I am unsure what.

Resist, Mellie! I yank away from him, not caring that his fingers are tightly wrapped in my hair, wanting the pain, needing it. But Helios is ready for the move, and he uses my momentum against me, spinning us so my back is pressed against the wall, his large body covering mine, pressing against mine, warming mine. Delicious. The thought bounces around my mind, and I try to catch it, needing to expel it, hating myself for even thinking it.

I shove at his chest, needing space. With him this close, I can't think. His scent envelops me, and though the madness is far away, I claw for it, desperate to escape this reality with him. I am aware that I'm on a timer. My resolve will only last so long.

The shove barely impacts Helios, and he continues to look down at me hungrily, smugly. I can tell he loves that I came here instead of to my own place. Motherfucker, why couldn't I have just gone home? He hovers his lips over mine, our breath mingling, and I suppress the shiver threatening to travel enticingly down my spine.

"Back the fuck up, Helios." I grind my teeth, trying to mask how my voice has lowered in need.

I shove uselessly at his chest again, but this time, he wraps his hands around my wrists, pinning them above my head. "No."

I snarl, but my chest heaves in anticipation of his touch. Searing heat encapsulates my wrist. It doesn't burn me, but I definitely feel it even after Helios lowers his hands. He smirks and my head snaps up when I try to put my arms down, and I can't. I find two glowing cuffs wrapped around my wrists. I pull at the restraints, but when I do, they get hotter and burn into my skin. The feeling is the sweetest of agonies and reminds me of Helios. Searing, delicious agony.

Helios drags the very tips of his fingers down the undersides of my arms, and I can't stop my shiver this time. His touch is so warm, and though I know he's not scorching my skin, his fingers feel blissfully smoldering.

"You going to keep fighting, hellcat?" he purrs. I meet his almost black gaze, and desire pools low in my stomach.

Fight this. I thrust my hips forward, trying to create a little bit of space by pushing him back.

"You trying to get my cock, gorgeous? You only have to ask." His seductive voice trails over me.

I pull harder on the restraints, not caring that they're burning me, leaning into the pain. Helios finally takes a step back, but it's not because he's retreating, not because I've won. He steps back and starts slowly unbuttoning his jeans. The sound of his zipper being dragged down is almost deafening, and I watch captivated. My breath leaves me in short pants, and my whole fucking body tingles in the way it only does before he touches me, before he fucks me.

He tilts his head at me. "You need me, hellcat?"

It takes a moment, a long moment, for me to clear my head enough to form a seething response, and it's an effort to push a snarl behind it to make it convincing. "Yeah, I need you. I need you to leave me the fuck alone."

Helios's lips curl. The smug fucker caught my struggle. His pants hang loosely on his hips, the base of his cock just barely visible, but the glaringly obvious bulge reveals what is otherwise hidden. He's hard as fuck. He starts to unbutton his shirt slowly, and I watch, unable to pull my eyes away as he reveals that mouthwatering chest. "Are you sure about that, Melinoë?"

Fuck… That fucking voice. I glide my tongue along my bottom lip as I imagine licking his chest. "I hate you." There is no malice in my voice, only tightly coiled desire.

Helios shrugs out of his shirt and lets it fall to the floor. My eyes seem spelled to his fingers, and I watch as he licks his forefinger, middle finger, and ring finger as he walks toward me. He takes a long, languid look at my lips as he slowly pushes his hand into my shorts. He's giving me time to tell him to stop, even though the bastard knows I can't. I can't deny him when he's this close and about to…

Fuck.

"Liar," Helios whispers smugly against my lips, his fingers grazing my pussy. He's barely touching me, but it's enough that he can feel how fucking wet I am for him. My torturous body bows to him as fucking usual. I bite back my moan, needing to withhold any additional satisfaction.

His eyes finally meet mine after trailing over every inch of my face, and something in them pulls me right into sanity, right into reality. There's a weird fluttering somewhere near my heart, and I panic. Something about being this close, about having him touch me like this in my moments of teetering, of anchoring myself to him like this, makes me need to escape. I need to get as far away from him as I possibly can. I pull on the restraints, cursing myself.

I don't want him. I don't want him. I don't want him. I try to use it as my mantra, but as his finger grazes my clit, my knees go weak.

Gods...

He's still looking at me in that way that makes me want to rip my heart out and plunge it into the deepest volcano. It would be destroyed forever but safe from him.

Nightmares. Use the nightmares.

I close my eyes and plunge myself into the realm of nightmares, not lingering for any longer than I need to. It is a dangerous place, horrific and unsurvivable. The darkness envelops me, and I shut my eyes tight. I hear the echo of a scream, and something shifts beneath me as I pay my penance for using this space. The second I am able to leave, I evaporate into smoke, appearing in my apartment.

I don't even take a moment to breathe before I rush to shut my blackout curtains and blinds, turning out all the lights. Helios cannot use his magic in the devouring darkness.

The bureau squeaks against the hardwood floor as I move it to barricade the front door. I expertly walk through my apartment in the darkness, going to the kitchen. My eyesight is better in the dark, honed after being stuck there for decades. I slide my hand along the countertop, stopping when I touch the knife block.

If Helios wants to come here, he'll be taking his life into his own hands. I wrap my hand around the cool steel of the handle, my bones shivering as I pull it free from the block. It rings lightly, shuddering as I drag it along the marble countertop. Then I wait, leaning against the kitchen door frame.

Less than thirty minutes later, I feel his presence outside my apartment. There is a slight tang of power, different from any of the divine assholes. I tilt my head, my gaze focused on the door, waiting to see what he will do next. I silently tsk and allow myself to bask in satisfaction as he turns the doorknob. Does he think I would make it so easy? My satisfaction is short-lived when I hear his steps retreat, followed by a large slam, the door groaning from the impact.

Stupid brute.

The first time he slams into it, the door barely moves in response. However, the door bulges inward when he hits it the second time. The legs of the bureau scrape against the wood, and when he hits it the third time, the door slams open, the bureau moving enough to permit him entry.

I stick to the shadows, sliding my fingers along the flat of the knife. My footsteps are nearly silent as I move around the perimeter of the room, keeping my eyes on Helios as he walks into the room. His rough curse is all I need to confirm my suspicions. His night vision is shit. Thought so. He thrives in sunlight, whereas the darkness coils around me like a lover, embracing both me and my madness, calling to it.

I continue my catlike movements around the room, slamming the door shut behind him. I hear Helios whirl on the spot, his eyes going to the now closed door. Any of the light from the hallway, now almost completely extinguished, save for a sliver creeping in beneath the door.

"You want to play hide and seek, kitten?" I can hear the frustration in his voice but also the anticipation of the challenge.

I press the knife's edge against the wall, dragging it against the wallpaper, uncaring whether I'm ruining the deep purple covering. It would look better with a couple of slashes and maybe some of Helios's blood.

"Come play," he croons, and I can hear the drain in his voice as he tries to use his glow. He won't manage it, though. In order to glow, you need a glimmer of light. There is no glimmer of light here. There is no glimmer of light within me, either.

Though his presence keeps me somewhat grounded, the darkness penetrates me, and I laugh at the feeling of it. Helios whips around in the other direction, facing the other way. I sneak up behind him, not touching him but stretching so my lips are at his ear.

"You shouldn't have come here, sunboy," I whisper. I reach up, pressing the knife to his throat. His pulse thrums beneath it, the blade twitching with every beat, but I don't sense any fear in him.

"What are you doing here?" I ask, tilting my head. I rub my body against his and press the blade a bit deeper into his skin, the sharp tang of his blood scenting the air.

"What do you think I'm doing here, kitten?" Helios growls softly.

I move around him, keeping the knife pressed against him. Once I am in front of him, I slowly drag the blade down his chest to the first button on his shirt. The point severs the thread, and the button drops to the floor. His chest heaves, the steel piercing his skin with every inhale. Still, there is no fear.

I continue moving the knife down, cutting button after button until they litter my floor. I tip my head, looking over his chest before leaning in and biting his pec.

Helios takes this as an invitation to grab my hips and pull me to him, groaning, "Hello, kitten."

In a flash, I press the knife to his throat again. I brush my lips over his skin and taste his thick, hot blood trickling down his chest. I let it cover my lips and chin.

"Are you afraid of the dark, sunboy?"

He squeezes my hip, pressing into the blade, and I shiver as I feel the sharp edge slice deeper into his skin. "Are you?" he asks, and there is such a depth to his voice that I have to bite back a moan.

I drag the flat edge down his chest, feeling each ridge of his muscles. "You shouldn't have come here."

Helios arches into the blade. "Why? Are you going to hurt me, kitten?"

I press the tip into one of his pecs, feeling the thrill as it pierces into him. "Yes." It's barely a whisper, barely a lie. I do want to hurt him, but not in the usual way.

Helios moans. The sinful noise makes me want to drop to my knees and worship him. "Good."

One word, one simple word, and my instinct to run disappears. Helios wraps his hand around mine and starts to drag the blade down. He pulls it away and takes it back to the beginning, drawing a diagonal line followed by another in the opposite direction. He guides my hand down, the blade sliding through his skin like it was water.

I look at the wound, his thick, sticky blood shining a little in the darkness, and I see the most perfectly imperfect "M" engraved in his absolutely perfect chest. The sight of it should repulse me. It should make me feel icky and gross, and I can't explain why, but I slam my lips to his. The taste of his blood is the first I get, coppery and with the tang of the Titans, but then his tongue collides with mine, and his taste overwhelms every fucking sense. I shove him down on the couch and lunge at him, straddling him, the knife still heavy in my hand.

My hands and body are covered in his blood, and I wrap my free hand around his throat, desperate for him. Helios groans into my mouth, his fingers digging into my hips almost painfully, and I want to scream at how good it feels. He rocks me against him, his hard length rubbing against my throbbing core. Helios rips my shorts from me as if they are made from nothing more than construction paper, and I moan as I bite his lip hard.

"Fuck, I hate you," I breathe into his lips. I feel him smile before he deepens the kiss.

"No, you fucking don't," he replies, lifting me so he can undo his pants.

Gods. I might actually die if he's not inside me within the next five seconds.

I shift my hips, helping him, and the second I feel his cock spring up, the tip pressing against my opening, I groan in need.

"You hate the way you want me," Helios growls, and I shut him up by slamming my hips down, taking his cock to the hilt.

"Don't want you." Why am I even lying about it? He is currently balls deep in me, and I'm not sure I've ever felt anything so exquisite.

"Tell that to your soaked cunt that's currently throbbing around my cock," Helios moans into my lips.

I groan and lift my hips. "Stop talking."

"Make me," Helios growls, grabbing my hips harder as he slams me down again, making me take him. He flips us, clearly wanting to be in control. He bucks his hips hard, his fingers bruising me.

I reach up, covering his mouth, though his words do nothing but spur me on, making me wetter for him. Helios bites my palm, and I arch beneath him. I don't fucking think so. I thrust my hips up, shoving him off the couch but going with him. I quickly shift so his cock is lined up again and slam my hips down, riding him hard and fast, desperate.

It doesn't last, though. Helios growls and rolls us again, our bodies hitting the coffee table. He shoves it out of the way, and it crashes against the wall, the glass ornaments smashing to the floor. He pins me to the ground and starts fucking me brutally into the floor, barely giving me space to arch for him. I dig my nails into his side, and he hisses. The split second of distraction gives me the upper hand, and I manage to get on top again, fighting him for dominance. The glass crunches beneath his body, and I feel it slice into my knees, but I don't fucking care.

Helios sits up, trying to regain some power, digging those scorching fingers into my hips, forcing me up and down on his cock.

I feel my orgasm building, a tight coil ready to spring. My whole body tightens in anticipation of the release. The sweet, sweet agony of pleasure, and the second Helios takes my nipple into his mouth, sucking once, I tumble over the edge and into the abyss.

Chapter Seven
Melinoë

NOTHING IN MY BODY IS STILL. My heart is racing, my chest is heaving, and every cell vibrates with satisfaction. Helios pants against my neck, his roar still ringing in my ears. I replay what we just did, and my muscles tense in pleasure with every wave of the memory.

It isn't until I open my eyes, the glow of his skin exquisitely burning my retinas, that I realize I had reined in my powers at some point. The penetrating black is no more, and Helios lights up the room like a beacon, his power drawing from the tiny sliver of light clawing its way in over the top of the curtains, desperate to enter now that my magic isn't dousing it.

Helios presses his lips to my shoulder, leaving a trail of kisses on my neck. My eyes roll, and I moan, tilting my head for him. The movement yanks me right back to reality, and I throw my body away from his, landing hard. Razor-sharp glass pierces my skin, the pain waking me even more. Shit.

"Melinoë!" Helios growls. "Be careful!"

The care in his words makes me numb to the pain. Just like always, my entire focus becomes him. No longer do I feel the sharp, jagged glass of the broken vase embedded into my thighs. There is only him, and it fucking infuriates me.

He scoops me up into his arms, shaking me slightly in an attempt to rid me of the glass. The musical tingle of the shards falling to the floor harmonizes with the sounds of our panting as we try to recover from the needs we just sated.

I meet his gaze, and the way his caramel-colored eyes hold mine makes my heart leap. I struggle in his arms, needing to get free of his touch.

"Leave," I grind out as I finally manage to get my feet on the ground and move away from him.

"Why?" I feel his gaze lock onto my back, my skin prickling beneath it.

"I don't want you here, asshole."

His answering scoff tells me he heard the falseness in my words. His hand brushes against the backs of my thighs, gently removing more of the glass. I grind my teeth at the way my skin tingles beneath his touch. "You trying to convince me or yourself, hellcat?" he asks, his voice like honey.

I snarl and bat his hand away, but it doesn't deter him. He continues to clear me of the tiny opaque daggers still piercing me.

"My kitty is so stubborn." I can hear the humor in his voice. He's enjoying this. Fucking weirdo.

I swat at him again and move away, walking toward my bedroom. "Leave. I need to prepare."

I hear him follow behind me, and the doorframe creaks a little as he leans his overly large body against it.

"Prepare?"

I dare to look at him and almost go to my knees at the sight. He leans in the doorway, exuding smug arrogance. His arms are crossed, making his biceps bulge in a way that would make a weaker goddess faint from the sight. But the thing that draws me to him the most at this moment, the thing that I'm struggling to resist, is the look in his eyes. He already knows what I need to prepare for. He's furious about it, and I know for certain that if I were to look closer and deeper into him, I would see the smallest sliver of the same madness that plagues me.

I purposely turn away and move to my wardrobe, pulling out all my clothes.

"Melinoë." I've never heard his voice so commanding, so domineering, and it makes my hair stand on the back of my neck. "Prepare for what?"

Don't look at him. Don't look at him. Don't look at him.

I throw item after item out of my closet. I toss them toward the bed but cast them so aimlessly that I'm certain they're missing their mark.

Helios grabs my arm, and I jump. I hadn't heard him

move closer. "Prepare for what?"

I snarl and bare my teeth at him, yanking my arm away.

He snarls back, crowding me, his huge body dwarfing mine. "Prepare. For. What?"

I smile wickedly at him. "None of your fucking business." I wave my hand, opening a black hole beneath his feet. He plummets into it, his roar making my smirk deepen as I close the hole.

I could have sent him somewhere dangerous, but honestly, it'll be more frustrating for him to just fall back into his own bed, knowing he can't use his powers to just flash back here. I'm about to use my magic to permeate the apartment with the unforgiving darkness, but Helios is too quick. He appears in a flash of light, and I curse.

There is no humor on his face, no smugness, only fury. I pick up one of my heels and throw it at him. He catches it easily. "Seriously?" he growls at me.

I throw another shoe, which he bats away. "Melinoë. If you're thinking of dreamwalking him—"

Ignoring him, I grab my journal from my bedside table and stomp back to the wardrobe, intent on climbing into it. I just need to get away from him. He yanks the journal from my hands, and I whirl on him, my fists clenched. He cannot read that journal. I summon it to me, and it turns into a searing shadow in his hands. It falls through his fingers, burning him as it does.

Helios hisses. "Seriously? What the fuck is in there?"

The journal drops into my waiting hands, and I scramble into the closet, closing the door and locking him out. Helios yanks on the handle, but it doesn't even rattle. I flick through the pages, finding the one I need. I place my palms on the worn paper and close my eyes, tilting my head back.

"Melinoë," Helios snarls, shaking the wardrobe, trying to open it. I ignore him and continue to concentrate. The darkness oozes from me, completely submerging me and the diary. Suddenly, I hear the shrill ring of a cell phone from outside the closet, and the shaking ceases.

"I have to go," Helios says. Something about the cadence of his voice makes me think it wasn't a call he was expecting, but I can't think about that now. I have to concentrate for Hades. For Persephone.

"About time, dickbag," I growl.

"Yeah, I'm here. Where are you?" His voice is retreating,

the concern in it clear. "I'll come meet you. Don't move."
I hear the latch click as my front door closes.

Chapter Eight

Helios

M Y FUCKING SISTERS ALWAYS SENSE THE WORST FUCKING TIME TO CALL ME. Like when I'm attempting to convince my girlfriend to let me be there when she dreamwalks her stubborn, adoptive father. I am not done fighting with Melinoë, and when I get back from this rather inconvenient summoning, I am going to insist. She's being an idiot by pretending I don't help her. A massive idiot. A massively violent and extremely hot idiot.

I flash into the bathroom of one of Selene's favorite haunts, a moonlight karaoke lounge. She has never been subtle. I wink at the man using the urinal as I step out of the stall. He gapes at my sudden appearance, trying to reconcile my presence with the previously empty bathroom. I roll my eyes. Mortals. He will concoct some excuse in his head, too much alcohol or the lighting. That is the thing I've learned while living among them for almost a thousand years. They didn't see shit, and when the Ancient Greeks died out, people became even more resistant to seeing anything out of the norm.

I pat him on the shoulder. "You're pissing on your feet, mate."

The guy jumps and looks down at his feet, seeing he is in fact doing just that, before adjusting his stream. I chuckle and rinse my hands off for show before heading into the lounge.

The mood lighting is way too dark and suggestive for the middle of the afternoon, but it's easy to spot the silver hair of my twin and the sunset hair of my other sister. I slide into the booth, looking between Selene and Eos. Selene and I share some similar features. We have the same lips and nose, but where I am gold, she is silver, from her hair to her eyes. Even her pale skin maintains a slight silver sheen. I've heard more than one mortal claim she must wear some type of body glitter.

Eos is her own personification, her hair is a cascade of colors, depicting every single color of the rising dawn. Her roots are a dark deep red, fading to orange and then yellow at the tips. Even her cheeks are constantly rosy, marking the blush of early morning. At first glance, none of us look related, our colorings too divergent from each other to mark us as siblings, but that's only at first.

"You made it sound like you were in trouble," I grumble to Eos, sliding into the secluded booth.

Eos blushes. "Well… we are, just not… well, right now."

I slide Selene's martini toward me and pop the olive into my mouth, ignoring her glare. "I was busy."

Selene narrows her eyes and crosses her arms. "With the nightmare goddess."

I chew the olive and swallow it loudly. "Melinoë."

Eos glances at Selene, shifting from side to side. "She has a lot of Olympian connections, doesn't she?"

I freeze, looking between my two sisters. This can't be good. I have a deal with Hades. We have a chosen side. Selene, Eos, and I made a pact after spending a thousand years imprisoned in Tartarus. We swore our loyalty to the Olympians in order to be released.

"We've spoken to Mother and Father," Selene adds, her voice as cool as the dark side of the moon.

Mother and Father? They hadn't spoken to us since we'd made the deal. They believed we were traitors for turning against our people. Eos reaches out and touches my hand, which I leave frozen on the table.

"They want to be a family again, like before the war," Eos pleads, her sunset eyes shimmering with sincerity and desperation.

"Are they planning to fight for the Olympians?" I ask, pulling my hand away from my sister's. Eos tries to mask her flinch but fails.

"No," Selene says. "Without the Primordials, you know the Olympians don't stand a chance against Kronos."

The treaty. Fuck. After another war of the Primordials threatened to start the world anew, a treaty was enacted. The Primordial Gods were bound to a stance of non-interference. They could not take a side or fight this time. I rub my brow, feeling the beginnings of a headache forming. I remember the last war. Fuck I'd been a general for them. I remember how the Olympians were losing. Kronos was about to extinguish them until Gaia stepped in. Once Gaia joined the fight, Nyx and Erebus followed. Without the Primes, the Titans may have the advantage once more.

"We gave up part of our abilities, Sel," I remind her. Apollo and Artemis now wield sway over the sun and the moon, though not to the level of true personification.

"Only part, Hel," she snaps back. She hated that she'd given up a part of her power, hated being even a little weaker than she once was. At the time, I would have given it all to get the fuck out of that prison.

Honestly, I probably still would under the right circumstances. Especially if it involved a goddess with dual-colored eyes. I mean, what had my abilities ever truly gotten me besides a role in a war I want no part in?

"You both want to side with the Titans?" I whisper, cautious of anyone close.

"We just… aren't sure," Eos responds, her voice shaking slightly. "I don't want to go back to Tartarus."

She rubs her hands over each other, trying to calm herself using her mantra and repetitive movements in order to relax.

"We need to be careful this time, and pick the winning side," Selene insists, not even bothering to mute her voice.

The winning side. That's fucking rich. When have I ever picked a winning side?

My eyes dart between them. "You mean you want me to pick the winning side."

They don't want to make the decision on their own, or bear the responsibility and repercussions of such a choice. They want me to shoulder the burden on my own. It was the same when we were young and even the deal for our freedom in Tartarus. It had to be my choice, my decision, my consequences.

Eos and Selene glance at each other, and though neither speaks, their silence confirms my suspicion.

I rub a hand down my face. "I'll think about it. I'll need some time."

"How much—" Selene starts.

"I don't know!" I snap and lunge to my feet. Closing my eyes, I exhale, reaching for patience. "I don't know. I'll call you."

My sisters look up at me, the silver moon and the burning dawn searing into my soul. The faith they have in me, and the responsibility they have forced onto my shoulders, are nearly unbearable.

"Thank you," Eos whispers, her eyes slightly teary.

I nod and walk away from them, flashing back to my flat as soon as I find a quiet spot. How can I choose a side?[7]

Chapter Nine

Helios

A MANIACAL LAUGH ECHOES BEHIND ME, AND I SPIN IN SURPRISE. My brow furrows. She came to me again. Even subconsciously. she knows we belong together. I step closer to her, worry filling me. She's curled into the wall with her knees drawn up against her chest, staring blankly at nothing.

"Melinoë?" I ask, holding out my hands, prepared for a feral launch from her. She must have fucking dreamwalked with Hades, despite my warning. I had only seen her like this after those times, but usually, even at her worst, she's aware that I'm present. Yet, when I kneel in front of her, her eyes are completely unfocused and glazed, and she's not wearing her glamor. Melinoë always wears her glamor over her scars in the mortal realm.

I gently grab her jaw. "Focus on me."

There is no awareness, only that continuing insane laugh. I'm not losing you to your mind, Melinoë. No matter what. You go only to places where I can follow. I pull back my hand and slap her hard. When her face turns toward me, I see a spiral of rage cut through the insanity, followed by flickers of the nightmares she's started conjuring around us. I blink, and when I open my eyes, she has shadowed away from me. I curse and stand, preparing to follow, when I hear her down the hall in my bedroom.

I walk past the nightmares painting the walls, ignoring the way they take physical form, trying to provoke me and draw me into the fear. Decaying hands reach out to brush me, to frighten me. I scoff, batting them away negligently. Nightmares don't have any effect on me. I can't sleep, so I can't dream. They have no power over me.

I push open the door to the bedroom, smirking when I see that Melinoë is not only in my bed, but she's buried her face into my pillow and is rubbing against it like a cat in heat. I tilt my head, watching her. She rubs her face in my scent, pulls away, and glances around vacantly. Then she remembers the pillow is there and buries her face into it again. It's just so fucking… cute.

I pull off my shirt, walking closer to her. She tightens her hold on my pillow and flashes her teeth at me, warning me off. Holding my hands up, I wait for her to relax before sliding into bed beside her. She lets out a low growl. I go still again, watching for her to forget about me and return to her pillow. It doesn't take long. Actually, it takes an insultingly short period of time for her to forget about me in favor of my pillow.

You're going to pay for that insult later, hellcat.

I slowly move closer, inch by inch. Each time I shift, Melinoë growls at me before forgetting and going back to the pillow. It takes over an hour before I'm able to replace the pillow with my chest, but when she buries her face against me, rubbing along me and purring happily, it is worth it.

Keeping my movements slow, almost hypnotic, I stroke her hair. That was the thing some people forgot about the sun. It could entice as well as warm. It could cause those fascinated with it to sear their eyes with its intensity from staring too long.

I know how much she likes the warmth, so I raise my body temperature slightly. Melinoë digs her nails into my stomach, and I muffle a moan. My body responds, eager for any pain inflicted by her, but this is not the time. She may have sought me out in this state, but she is hardly aware.

"I'm here," I whisper, keeping my body heated to a comforting temperature.

Melinoë tenses the second I speak, and I silently curse myself. Why couldn't I just keep my mouth shut?

She pulls back after a moment, glaring at me with still-vacant eyes. Her pupils have consumed the gray of one eye and the other completely unbroken black. A growl rips from her, making her sound closer to a beast.

I blink in surprise before growling back, just as feral and fearsome. We are two monsters greeting each other in the dark.

Melinoë pauses, cocking her head to the side as if trying to understand who and what I am. She studies me for a moment before hissing softly and curling back into me, her nails digging into my stomach. She's always pinning me, clinging to me as if I'm on the brink of leaving her. Or maybe she considers me prey that she's loathe to relinquish.

I'm not sure how much time passes before she relaxes into me. Her body melts against mine, and I close my eyes, simply enjoying the moment with her. I wish she would seek this from me fully sane. Yet, at the same time, I prefer that she does it when she's past the brink because it makes it completely undeniable. When she's at her most vulnerable, she looks for me. I'm her shelter, even when she can trust nothing. When her own mind turns against her, I'm her safety.

She nudges insistently at my jaw with her nose, clearly wanting something from me. I look down at her, and she presses her lips softly to mine. This kiss is different from all our others. This kiss is sincere and vulnerable, two things she never allows herself to be around me. It's a kiss full of broken promises and pain too intense to speak of. It speaks of the horrors she can conjure but experiences herself at the same time, of all the things she's yet to share with me, and of all the things about her I can't wait to know.

She whimpers softly, deepening the kiss for a moment before pulling away. I bury her face against my neck, wondering how long she'll be in this state of partial awareness. It doesn't truly matter. I'll wait in the abyss with her until she's ready.

Chapter Ten
Melinoë

Falling.

I'm falling into the abyss, and there is nothing I can do. I see nothing but colors spinning in front of me, but the darkness swallows them one by one. Over and over. Once there is nothing but black left, shapes come toward me.

Home. I need to get home.

The blade is pressed to my thigh, blood trickling from the wound. There is no pain, only warm stickiness. My face is pressed into a forge over and over, the stone glowing red from the heat.

I was born to be hurt. It is all I am here for.

"Little Melinoë. How pretty you bleed. Look at those hideous scars. You are my canvas," a voice crows from my memory.

A laugh spins around my head as if circling a drain, getting closer and closer, unbearably loud as it passes my ears.

I glance at my hand. It's bright pink dotted with purple polka dots, and I'm holding a balloon. The string weaves through my fingers, and I follow it with my eyes to the top. I expect to see the helium-filled rubber, but there is no balloon at the end of the string. Instead, there is a severed head. I release the string, and the head falls at my feet with a sickening thud. I reach out and push at it lightly, shuddering at the feel of the cool, waxy flesh against the pads of my fingers.

"Hey!" the head snarls, long fangs shooting from its gums.

I shuffle away and fall off a ledge, falling once more. Hands shoot out from the invisible walls, all at different stages of decay, reaching for me. I see one that I recognize.

They are large with tanned, soft skin. I catch the scent of sunlight and coconut, the slightest shred of light coming from below. I reach for the tanned hand, but I'm grabbed by the throat. Gangrenous fingers squeeze my airway, and I struggle in their hold. I wrap my hand around the wrist, but my grip slips and I only succeed in pulling a flap of skin free.

The light is gone now. There is only darkness and the lingering phantom smell of… something I need.

"N-need light," I grate out, struggling for air. Though even if I do free myself, where to next? Maybe a field of blood-thirsty vampires is my next destination, or maybe a pigpen full of zombified farm animals.

Light shoots into the blackness, piercing the depths and turning everything within it to dust. I wait to start falling again, but I'm wrapped in a cocoon of warmth reminiscent of the most loving embrace.

"… don't know if this will help…"

The voice adds itself to the cacophony in my mind, but it's not one that I am familiar with. None of my voices have names, but I can tell them apart by the horrors they speak and the instructions they give. This isn't one of them. This voice is deep, warm, and soothing.

My whole body lurches, my head snapping back as I push against the light. The insanity croons to me, but it is nothing compared to the sinful voice of the light tugging me toward it. The warmth envelops me, and I rise, no longer falling through the despair and nightmares. This time, I am passing through the ashes of unfulfilled dreams.

I gasp, nothing but warm light filling my vision. Yet, it's not blinding. Everything is so fucking clear. The light dims ever so slightly, and I look up, meeting the concerned caramel eyes of Helios.

Helios.

I can't look away, my gaze glued to his. His light pierces my brain, keeping it stable, keeping me here with him. Slowly, I lift my hands and wrap my fingers around Helios's wrists, pulling them away from my temples. The light in the room dulls, only coming from the two small table lamps on either side of the bed.

I'm about to shove his hands away from me, but at the last second, I place one of them on my hip, needing his touch to ground me. Helios releases a shaky breath, his thumb softly sliding along the exposed skin of my waist. He leans down, hovering his lips over mine, and I can see the relief in his eyes. Worse, I can see something else there.

Something I'm desperate not to see.

"This never happened," I whisper against his lips. Our breath mingles into the most potent lust potion.

Helios's eyes sparkle a little, the challenge spurring him on. "Why? Scared?"

Fucking terrified.

Why the fuck had I come here? How did I end up in his bed? How did he pull me from that? Previous to this, an episode that bad would have taken me months to pull myself out of, and then it would have taken as many months to get over the terror of it.

I swallow, glancing at his lips, then slowly let my gaze trail up his face until I meet his dark gaze. Too much, there is too much in those eyes. It's too much for me to handle.

"See ya." I wink at him and disappear from his bed, leaving behind a puff of black smoke and sexual frustration.

No sooner am I back in my home than my phone beeps. I already know it's him, and I slump down on my couch before grabbing my phone.

HELIOS

How many times are you going to pretend like there's nothing going on between us?

MELLIE

There is nothing between us.

I'm not sure that's true anymore, but I'm not going to tell him that.

HELIOS

You came to me. Twice.

I see the little text bubble bobbing up and down. Fuck this. I block his number and turn my phone off, slamming it down on the table. What the fuck does Helios know?

My thoughts are still on Helios as I stomp through my apartment, taking out leftover frustration on my wood flooring.

"You came to me," I repeat, mimicking his stupid honey voice. Yeah, only cause I'm insane.

Along with the anger at myself and Helios, I am bone tired, and by the time I'm pulling on my pajamas, sleep is tugging at me.

Usually, after an episode like tonight, not only would I be stuck in my insanity for an undetermined amount of time, but I'd also be exhausted when I eventually came out of it. Both because when I am lost among the nightmares, I cannot lose myself into unconsciousness to rest, and because my nightmares tend to manifest themselves into reality. In that state, I don't even notice, never mind ward them off.

I fall into bed, my muscles groaning as they collide with the soft mattress. Something in my stomach twists at the lack of sunshine and coconut scent against the pillow. I'm about to threaten it with violence, but sleep swallows me whole.

DION SNORTS A LINE OF AMBROSIA OFF A WOMAN'S ABDOMEN, GESTURING FOR ME TO JOIN IN. I wave my hand, declining. I'm not interested in that kind of fun. Stupidly, I came to Dion's club in search of... something. Alright, I'll admit it. I came to Dion's club because not only is he the God of Wine, but he's also the God of Madness. For some reason, I thought being around another batshit crazy god would be soothing and as close as I can get to the one I really want. Who, I am pretending, has zero effect on me. I don't know who the fuck I am fooling, definitely not myself.

Dion rubs his nose and leans back, his eyes already clearing. The secret of Dion is that he's always mad, but under certain drugs and drinks, he actually becomes sane. There is a rumor of a mortal who might have the same effect on him, someone who brings the God of Madness clarity, but he hasn't confirmed or denied it.

"You know, I didn't expect a Titan to visit me," Dion drawls. His voice is like honeyed wine sliding down the back of your throat. "Given current events."

Current events. Fuck, can I go anywhere without hearing about this fucking war?

"It has nothing to do with me," I reply cooly, turning the glass in my hand. It was empty except for three melting ice cubes, and I'd turned down several refills. Instead, I am just holding the glass to have something to do with my hands.

"You're a Titan," Dion adds, dropping his head back slightly on the upholstered booth, no doubt the ambrosia taking effect.

"So they tell me."

Dion laughs, and it grates my nerves. It's not the right

laugh. It doesn't sound like Melinoë's melodic witch cackle that definitely frightens small children and conjures up the image of a demonic creature peeling the skin from someone's bones.

I put my glass down and stand. "Thanks for the drink."

Dion smirks. "You know, most people talk to me when they come to the club. I'm a great listener."

I wave at him over my shoulder, not looking back as I head home. Or at least I intend to head home, but somehow, I find myself outside Melinoë's apartment, breaking her lock. I could use the key I had made, but I want her to know I was here. I step instead and head for her bedroom, crossing my arms over my chest when I see her empty bed. Where is she? She wouldn't be out... on a date? No. Definitely not.

My keys jangle as I flip them over my finger repetitively, taking the long way home. I unlock and swing my door open, my brows shooting up in surprise when her familiar scent hits me. Is that left over from earlier? No, it's too fresh. I follow it to my bedroom, standing in the open door, blinking stupidly at Melinoë curled form on my bed.

What is she doing here? Her bed is empty, and she came to mine? I rub my chest, my heart aching at the thought. She is looking for me more and more. How much longer is this going to last? Did she choose to come to me? Or was she already asleep when she did?

Either way, she'd bail the second she woke up. My eyes narrow on her, and I decide not this time. I flash away to one of the bolt holes I have hidden all around the world. Smirking, I grab the black adamantium cuff and flash back. I snap it closed around her ankle and nod in satisfaction. Let's see her shadow away now.

I strip down into my briefs and crawl into bed with her. Her nose wrinkles in sleep, and she twitches before pressing herself against me. She buries her face into my chest, searching out my warmth, and I keep my body at the perfect temperature, lulling her deeper into a peaceful sleep.

Her brow crinkles and I trace the line across her forehead. What does the Goddess of Nightmares dream of? She's not having a nightmare, at least not like she had before when she started conjuring terrors.

"What is it about you that has me so... captivated?" I whisper, watching her.

She wrinkles her nose again, and I smile before I pick up my phone, distracting myself as she sleeps. Hours pass before she stretches against me.

"Morning," I say, tossing my phone aside.

She groans but doesn't open her eyes. "Why are you here?" Even as she asks, she curls her nails into my chest, loath to part with her prize.

I smirk. "You mean my own bed?"

She opens her eyes and sits up. "You fucking kidnapped me from my apartment? Fucking weirdo."

"You came here." I grin and blow her a kiss. "Again."

She glares at me, her eyes still clouded with sleep. "Enjoy your delusion."

Melinoë scowls, and her form flickers as she tries to shadow. She blinks and tosses the sheets off, looking down at her ankle. Her mouth drops open. "Are you fucking kidding me?" She jumps to her feet. "You kidnapped me and put me on fucking solar-stalker house arrest?"

I prop myself up on my elbows. "I didn't kidnap you."

She snarls. "Take the cuff off."

"No."

She lunges, straddling me. "Fucking remove it now."

Immediately rock hard. Damn, what is it about her violent nature that turns me to stone? This was what I was searching for by going to Dion's club, but nothing can compare to this raw, feral creature threatening to kill me.

She grabs my face, pulling me closer. "Why won't you leave me alone?" Her eyes dart between my eyes and my lips. "Why am I here?"

She asks the question so softly that I don't think she meant to say it out loud.

"Because you needed me," I whisper. "And you're afraid of what that means, how you—"

She slams her lips to mine, stopping my words. I growl into her mouth and bite her lip, pulling back before releasing it. "This won't change anything. You'll still need me after."

"Stop talking," she snarls, digging her fingers into my hair.

"Make me."

She slams her mouth to mine again, our teeth clashing. I rip her shirt down the middle and toss it aside before moving on to her sleep shorts and panties. I don't break the kiss, even as I shove my briefs down for her. She tugs at my hair hard enough to pull out a chunk.

"Say you need me," I growl into her mouth.

She glares at me. "No."

I fist her hair, yanking it hard. "Why?"

"Why the fuck does it matter?" she growls.

"It matters because you're lying." I slam my lips to hers. "Lying to me." I kiss her harder. "Lying to yourself."

She shoves me back onto the bed, breaking the kiss. Her breath is jagged and sharp, the tatters of her pajamas barely clinging to her.

"Fight it all you want, but you come to me in your sleep and when you're on the brink because you need me."

And I need you.

Chapter Twelve
Melinoë

I SHOVE HIS LARGE, STUPID BODY OFF ME AND CLIMB OUT OF HIS BED, cursing myself once again for coming here. While it's entirely possible Helios kidnapped me, and the cuff around my ankle would evidence this, I know it was my traitorous body that brought me here to him. I'm going to have to chain myself to my own fucking bed to prevent this from happening again. It makes that glowing dickbag altogether too happy.

"What's the point of running?" Helios growls as I near his bedroom door. I grab one of his T-shirts, needing something a little more substantial to brave the crisp air of wintertime in the city.

"What's the point in any of this, Helios?" I ask, loving the way my mouth curls around his name.

Helios kneels on the edge of his large bed and grabs my arm, his eyes soft, looking up at me almost pleadingly. He needs to fucking stop it.

"I like you," he says, the words filling the room, taking up every scrap of air. His eyes do that insufferable twinkle that I'm growing so used to. He knows the impact his words have on me, and I need to take the power back. Right the fuck now.

I narrow my eyes at him. "Well, I think you're a UV dumbass with lava for brains," I retort, able to hear the petulance in my voice.

Helios yanks my arm, pulling me closer and sitting up on his knees. It's so unfair that he's still taller than me. He always has the high ground.

"Are you flirting with me, Melinoë?" His eyes glimmer

as his lips tug into his signature smirk.

Why does he like my cruel words? My insults? I pull my lips into a snarl, baring my teeth. "I would rather plunge myself into the fiery depths of the actual sun."

Helios groans, his eyes darkening. "I can arrange that, hellcat."

"Fucking weirdo," I growl back, my stomach fluttering.

Helios shifts off the bed. Towering over me, he crowds me, pushing me back until I feel the wall behind me.

"Insult me more," he demands, his voice low with lust.

"Don't tell me what to do, dick for brains."

Helios lets out a low moan, planting his hands on either side of my head and looking down at me. "So sexy. Fuck."

I shove at his chest and force myself to hold his gaze. I will not let my eyes wander to those full lips that taste like the most perfect summer evening.

"You are so fucking annoying," I growl, pushing at his chest again. He barely moves from the impact. "I hate you," I add for an additional flourish.

Helios moves in closer, his body dwarfing mine. He presses me against the wall, enveloping me in his heat, his scent. He rocks his hips against me, and when I feel his boner rub against my stomach, every nerve inside me becomes alert, tense, and desperate. It's fucking embarrassing.

"More…" Helios grates out, rocking his cock against me again. My heart thunders in my chest, my breasts brushing against his chest with every inhale.

"You're so…" I pant. "So…" I snarl and slam my lips to his, giving into my animalistic urge to kiss him, touch him.

Helios doesn't wait for permission. He groans low and deepens the kiss, sliding his tongue against mine, tasting me. The sound sends a wave of uncut desire through my entire body, and all I can think about is how we're not close enough. We will never be close enough. He slides his hands down my body and cups my thighs. He lifts me, and I immediately wrap myself around him. I bite his tongue and twine my fingers into his hair, yanking it hard.

Helios briefly moves one of his hands from my thigh, and I'm about to protest when he slams his cock into me. The scream that rips from my throat belongs to him, and I am so fucking glad of that. Helios growls into my mouth, thrusting relentlessly. His fingers dig into my thigh, my pussy throbbing with the knowledge that I will wear his mark. His fingertips bruised into my flesh will remind me that while he is the most infuriating being I have ever had the misfortune of meeting, he also makes me feel things

I never thought I could, never thought I would. Helios is pure euphoria and clarity.

Helios slams into me, the wall at my back groaning with the force of his thrusts. Pleasure surges through me each time he plunges his thick cock into me. Helios pulls back, still fucking me mercilessly. He watches me, his eyes black and feral, as he wraps his hand around my throat and squeezes lightly.

Never would I let just anyone at my throat, but I trust Helios. I hate that I trust him, but I do. My lips part slightly as he tightens his hand on my neck. I gasp, trying to draw in whatever air I can. His gaze roams over my face, searching for something. Whatever it is, he seems to find it. He loosens his hold a little, allowing me to breathe again, and I gulp the oxygen down, my lungs burning with it.

Helios drops his hand, his eyes softening as he meets my gaze again. My heart sputters from the look in his eyes, and I grab his face roughly. I need more from him, but most of all, I need that look to go away because I can see lo— No!

"Harder. Fucking ruin me," I snarl, though my subconscious chuckles. He has already fucking ruined me.

Suddenly, Helios pulls out of me, and my pussy clenches at the emptiness, throbbing from the feeling of pleasure being ripped away so unexpectedly. Helios doesn't give me a chance to protest. He spins me away from him and presses my cheek against the wall, his fingers clenching in my hair as he plunges into me again from behind. "Shut the fuck up."

I brace my hands against the wall, my whole body tensing in exquisite pleasure. Helios is even deeper inside me, and his growls at my ear send a surge of need between my legs with every thrust. His hand tightens in my hair, my scalp burning as he yanks my head to the side. I moan, and he slams his lips to mine, kissing me desperately.

I dig my nails into the wall and feel the paint curl under my nails. Helios slides his lips to my neck, licking once over my pounding pulse before biting me hard. His teeth sink so deep into my skin that my head spins from the delicious agony of it.

My cries of pleasure and the sounds of him plunging into my soaked core fill the room. The wall shakes as Helios brutally fucks me into it, and my eyes roll in pleasure at the thought of us fucking destroying the structural integrity of his bedroom.

"Helios, cut me," I moan. It's my voice, but the words sound like they're coming from far away. All I want, all I need, is for him to slice into my skin. I need to feel the pain of something slashing against me. Helios drags his nails down my back, and I scream. My back bows, pushing my hips harder against him, taking him deeper.

"Say my name as you come, kitten," Helios moans into my neck.

I groan, arching more, feeling my ichor trickle down my sides. "No."

"I'll stop," Helios hisses.

Stop? Oh fuck no. I snarl, shoving back against him, meeting every brutal thrust, feeling my orgasm approaching.

"If you stop, I'll make you regret it."

Helios stops and steps back, pulling out of me. I whirl to face him. His arms are crossed over his chest, his cock standing thick, proud, and covered in my arousal. The sight is so damn erotic, I whimper. Fuck. I shove him down on the bed, straddling him.

"Say my name," he growls up at me, grabbing my hips and rolling us so he's on top. "Say it, and I'll give you what you need."

"You're not in charge here, sunboy."

Helios grabs my wrists, pinning them above my head. He shifts and rocks his cock against me, the tip grazing my clit maddeningly.

"Fuck, my girl is so wet," he moans. He looks down at me, and I can see the desire in his eyes.

"I'm thinking of someone else," I lie. "And I'm not your girl." I lift my hips, trying to lock the tip of his cock at my entrance, needing relief.

"Let me guess. You're thinking of the Titan of the Sun?" He bucks his hips, denying me, and my clit throbs in need. "Say my name."

"Hel—"

He moans, "Come on, baby, almost there."

"Hell no," I growl. "Fuck me."

Helios smirks, bending down to bite my neck. "Say. My. Name."

I moan, the desire too much. It's physically painful. "Fuck. Helios."

His groan is a reward itself, but I barely register it before he thrusts inside me. "That's right, baby."

I yank against his hold on my wrists, wanting to touch him. He releases them and rolls us, letting me take control. I sit up on him and waste no time in riding him, slamming my hips against him over and over.

"Fuck, you're so sexy," he groans, and I feel his gaze locked on me. "Hit me."

I look down at him and slap him across the face hard. His head snaps to the side, and when he looks up at me, I realize I've never seen him truly feral until this moment. Helios bucks his hips beneath me, pushing deeper inside me. My cunt clamps down hard on his cock, and he reaches up and slaps me, not quite as hard as I hit him, but hard enough that my cheek sings from his palm. The pain travels through my body, and I move faster on him, bouncing on him, desperate for more.

"Fuck, I hate you."

"Then fuck me like it," Helios groans.

Scooping the remnants of my panties from the bed, I stuff them into his mouth. The black lace against his lips may just be the single most erotic thing I have ever seen. He digs his fingers into my hips, and I know I will wear his bruises.

"Don't you look pretty with my panties stuffed in your mouth?" I ask, dragging my nails down his chest and over his abs. I grab his wrists and pin them above his head, looking down at him. His gaze sears into me, his eyes glowing with need and fury.

"Pretty and at my mercy." I fuck him harder, riding him faster. His cock throbs inside me, driving me wild.

"Fuck. Fuck, fuck, fuck. Why do you feel so fucking good?" I groan, getting close. My orgasm burns at the base of my spine, and I can already tell it's going to wreck me. Helios just continues to look up at me, taking me in, letting me take what I need from him.

My orgasm comes hard, and just as expected, it obliterates everything inside me. I arch, screaming his name as my cunt clamps down on his length.

Helios's roar is muffled by my panties as he comes, but it still manages to shake me to my core.

My hips slow as waves of pleasure cascade through me, my body quivering. I roll off him, panting. Helios pulls my panties from his mouth and yanks me back to him. He presses soft kisses over my face and tenderly caresses me. The contrast between these gentle touches and the brutality of our coming together makes my belly clench. The feeling of his release spilling out of me just increases the continuing sweet agony of my post-orgasmic bliss.

I swat at him weakly, my heart thundering in my chest. "That was the last time," I promise, sending it out into the universe once again.

Helios continues to kiss and nuzzle me. Idiot. I bat him away again, relieved when I hear his phone pinging.

"Saved by the bell. I have to split anyway." I sit up, shifting out of his embrace. Helios easily pulls me back, kissing me hard, passionately. I find myself kissing him back, and I give myself a shake, pushing him away again.

Helios tugs me back once again. "Stay."

"No," I growl, crossing my arms.

"Yes," Helios growls back.

"I'm not staying, Helios," I insist, but I can feel sleep tugging at me again, still exhausted from the dreamwalking, from the insanity, from the fucking.

Helios kisses my cheeks, eyes, and nose, and I swear I feel him getting warmer. The bed seems to become impossibly comfortable beneath me.

"Leaving…" I growl, but then I fall into sleep, surrounded by a cloud of sunlight.

I SETTLE INTO BED AND KISS HER HEAD BE-FORE GRABBING MY PHONE TO ORDER HER FAVORITES FOR DELIVERY. Ghost pepper chili, tiger sushi, black bun burger, squid ink pasta, all the spiciest, and anything dyed an unusual color. I flash the food to my nightstand once it's dropped off, refusing to move from this spot, enjoying every second she's pressed against me. An hour later, she scrunches her nose and digs her nails into my stomach again. Another thing I love. I'm tempted to get tattoos in the shape of her nails on my stomach. Hmm, that actually sounds like a great idea. I should put it on my to-do list.

"Helios," she mumbles, and I lower my phone, forgetting completely about my to-do list. She consumes me completely. The sun might be the center of this universe, but mine is here, in bed with me.

"Yes, baby?" I murmur, seeing her eyes aren't even open, her voice still drugged with sleep.

Her nose twitches. "Love."

An hour later, I open one of the containers of food, allowing the scent to waft over us. Melinoë's stomach rumbles, and her fingers tighten on me before she opens one eye. I hold up a box of firecracker shrimp. She takes the box and snatches the chopsticks, growling softly, "Why are you always here?"

I smother a smile as she stretches and sits up before starting to eat. "You mean at my flat?"

Melinoë grumbles and gets out of bed. Naked and still eating the shrimp, she heads toward the door. I blink and get up to follow after her. "Where are you going?" She doesn't answer, and I catch her around the hips before she can open the door. "Hey." She takes an aggressive bite of shrimp before looking up at me, menace in her eyes. I kiss her, licking some of the spice lingering on her lips. "Why don't you stay and eat all the food I ordered?" Her eyes narrow. "If you eat it all, then I won't have any more food."

That was the thing about Melinoë. She would only stick around if it meant I was deprived of something. If she eats all my food, then I won't have food.

"I'm leaving," she insists.

I pick her up and turn around, heading back toward the bed, even as she struggles against my hold. "Stay." I take the food from her hand and set it aside before pushing her back onto the bed. She snarls at me, but the bags under her eyes are even more apparent. I lean down and cup her cheeks. "You haven't been sleeping."

She swats my hands away. "Ugh, stop with the mushiness."

I smile at her and immediately put my hands back. "Eat. Sleep. And I won't be mushy for the next twenty-four hours."

"And you'll leave me alone?"

"Once I'm satisfied, you will get a Helios free twenty-four hours." I roll my shoulders. "Though that also means twenty-four hours without the best sex of your life, so…"

She rolls her eyes. "Calm down, you're average."

I laugh and crawl onto the bed, kissing her hard. "I'm the best, and you know it." I lick my lips. "I can still taste your pussy," I moan, "and your panties."

She hisses and shifts beneath me. "I will eat and sleep for another few hours, and then I want forty-eight hours."

I ignore her stipulation, pretending I agree by shifting to lie next to her. I turn on the television and lean back against the headboard. She moves away from me, sitting as close to the edge of the bed as possible. She picks up the firecracker shrimp and inhales it before moving on to the next carton of squid ink pasta.

"Hate you," she tosses at me, her mouth full of food.

When was the last time she ate? When she has her episodes, does she remember to eat? Or even sleep?

"No need to pretend. Everyone here knows the truth," I drawl. "You're obsessed with me."

She hisses as she finishes the pasta and starts on the burger. "I will call off this deal."

I glance at her and turn the channel to HGTV. She pauses mid-bite, her brows furrowing. I wink at her. "It's your favorite."

"You're a creepy weirdo stalker." She curls up slightly, still eating. "I fucking love home renovation shows."

I shift closer as the show continues. Melinoë squeals as a wrecking ball takes down a building. She moves closer, and I pull her against my side. She is so distracted she barely notices. I wonder if she only likes the destruction part of the show, yet when they start decorating, she looks just as captivated.

She slowly leans against me, and I wrap my arm around her tightly. "They should have picked the other house."

"Please!" she says. "They are getting way more for their money there. Plus, they have a huge scope to extend!"

I knew she loved the show but underestimated how deep she gets into the stories. "But the other one had the beach view!"

"Constantly trailing sand through the house, please!" She glares at me, even as she finishes the last of the takeout. "You really do have lava for brains."

A new episode starts, and we continue watching. The show is almost mind-numbing but engaging, and through it all, we continue our volley of commentary. "How do they afford a quarter million working as a contractor?" "Why the fuck would you paint that room lavender?!" "Mermaids are stupid. Sirens are much cooler." The last was about an eleven-year-old's bedroom design.

"I think having everything dark and closed makes it easier to pretend you're alone," I add, as she critiques an open floor plan, demanding dark and shadowy.

"I don't care what you think." She pouts. "Dick."

I snicker at her, even as she growls at me and heads for the bathroom. I take the brief intermission and toss out the takeout containers, waiting for her to return.

Chapter Fourteen
Melinoë

I GAZE AT MY REFLECTION IN THE MIRROR, my attention zeroing in on my eyes. Since Helios gave me that injection of light straight into my grey matter, everything has been pretty quiet in there. I still feel the tug of insanity. It's ever-present, but I know I'm not in imminent danger of nose-diving into it. I'm not sure I've ever been at this point before. The tightrope seems to have expanded slightly, and now I can fit my entire foot on the iron rope.

I brush my fingers over the invisible scars marring the left side of my face. They always feel more sensitive after I've been trapped within my mind. That whole side of my face throbs dully, reminding me that while I might be sane right now, I shouldn't get complacent. The madness still resides within me. It always will.

I turn the tap on, splashing some cold water on my face, and it burns the ruined skin hidden beneath my glamour. Through the door, I can hear Helios moving around in the bedroom. No doubt he is attempting to make the room nice for me to return to.

Why does he have to be so fucking considerate?

The bathroom matches the aesthetics of his apartment, all terracotta and boho. It would look better if it were dark and mysterious. Some people have no taste.

Not feeling ready to go back to him yet, I have a quick look through his medicine cabinet. I roll my eyes at all the expensive colognes, vitamins, and moisturizers. I've definitely seen some of this stuff in Persephone's vanity. The cuff on my ankle pinches at my skin, anger throbbing through my body with the reminder. Mumbling a few curses, I grab the small wicker wastebasket and dump all his toiletries into it.

The hidden scars continue to throb, the discomfort increasing in intensity to the point that I want to rip off that side of my face. Cold water is the only thing that seems to help in this situation, and the colder, the better. If I could plunge myself into a glacier, I would. I climb into the shower and turn it on. The icy spray makes me shiver, but after the initial burn of it against my cheek, it begins to soothe the pain.

I sigh in relief and close my eyes. My lips twitch when Helios steps in behind me and yelps. His heat fills the space, but it only makes the water feel colder and more delicious against my skin. I roll my head back at the feeling, losing myself in it. Helios's warm skin presses against mine as he wraps his arms around me, the water hissing as it collides with the inferno that is his bronzed skin.

Helios brushes his lips over my cheeks, and the difference in temperature makes me shiver with desire. I don't push him away, loving the sensation of his skin against my back, contrasting with the shockingly cold water. He runs his fingers through my hair, massaging my scalp. I don't even try to stop the purr that escapes me as I relax into it. The smell of coconut is so strong in this flawless glass prison, and some sick part of me basks in the idea that I'll smell like him.

He continues to wash my hair, and I moan. I chance a glance at him, expecting to catch him staring at me, but he is absorbed in his task. His eyes are glued to my hair, his fingers expertly massaging my scalp and lathering the shampoo.

I turn to face him and brush my fingertips along his bottom lip, fascinated by how it drags to the slide slightly before bouncing back. Helios doesn't seem to notice, tipping my head back to rinse the shampoo. I search his face, confused about why he didn't react to me, but he simply grabs the conditioner and applies it to my wet hair.

After another rinse, he carefully washes my entire body with a stone-colored loofa before finally meeting my gaze. Not a word has been spoken between us. No snarky remarks, no threats, and no smug declarations. Simply him and me, naked, vulnerable, and raw. I step out of the shower, wrapping a towel around me.

What the fuck was that?

The ache in my face is long forgotten, and I pull on one of his shirts before falling into bed. I glance at the bedside table, surprised to see my phone. Helios must have grabbed my phone from my place.

I prop myself up on my elbows and open my messages with Persephone. Even knowing she won't receive the message, I start to type. I want to talk to her so badly. She understood me, and she'd been there for me from the moment we met. Loved me.

MELLIE

So, Helios is the worst. And he keeps doing all of these cute things and I hate it so much. It makes my stomach flutter in the worst way imaginable. I need you to come back now because I hate him and I miss you. Hades doesn't get it. Plus he's boring as fuck. Anyway, if I nap for a bit longer, Helios is going to leave me alone for forty-eight hours so that's a huge win. Love you, P.

The phone makes a small whooshing noise as the message shoots to Persephone's phone, and I feel lighter, having sent her my thoughts.

Helios comes back through, and I lock my phone, glancing at him over my shoulder. His eyes are soft, and those annoying feelings are shining in them. The sand-colored towel is slung low around his hips, and I force myself to keep my gaze locked on his. He tugs the comforter, covering me up, and then walks to his closet to change. He emerges and smirks at me as he slips beneath the covers on the other side of the bed, propping his pillows up behind him.

I narrow my eyes at him. "So, I sleep for a couple of hours," I begin, "and I don't hear from you or see you for forty-eight hours."

Helios grabs a book from his bedside table. "Twenty-four," he says nonchalantly.

I sit up. "No. We agreed on forty-eight."

He quirks a brow. "I did not agree to it."

I growl and climb out of bed, but like a tentacled octopus, he grabs me and pulls me back to him.

"How about twenty-four, and I take the cuff off?"

That slippery little eel. I'd forgotten about the cuff. I knew it meant I couldn't use my powers to escape him, but could it also have a tracker? Or an enchantment that would make me pine for him, longing for him for every second we are apart?

"Thirty-six. And you take the cuff off." I throw back, my eyes narrowed.

"Twenty-five," he counters.

"Thirty-three."

"Twenty-three."

"Thirty."

"Twenty-three."

I roll my eyes. "Okay, bye. Whatever." I climb out of bed, but Helios grabs my arm, holding me there.

"Twenty-eight," he growls. "Final offer."

I glance at him, considering. Twenty-eight is better than nothing. It'll give me some clarity from him. Some space to be free of the brain fog he causes. While he may chase away the insanity and the nightmares, there's a light pink hue that always seems to cloud my brain when I'm with him. It's annoying. It makes colors brighter, and things taste better. Helios strokes my arm with his thumb, distracting me.

"Twenty-eight and you'll remove the cuff."

He nods, his eyes locked on mine, dancing with the thrill of the verbal battle he loves to engage in with me. "Deal." Helios's smile brightens his face, his skin glowing with happiness.

I roll my eyes and climb into bed, lying down. "But no sex."

His laugh brushes down my spine. "No sex?"

I glare at him, yanking the pillow beneath my head, trying to give the illusion that I'm not already comfortable.

"Did you want me to push for it?" he asks, his eyebrow raised.

"Whatever." I close my eyes passive-aggressively.

Helios merely tucks me in, kissing me softly on the head. I roll onto my other side, giving him my back. I feel Helios's fingers trailing over the nape of my neck, and I shiver at the feeling of his touch. He pushes the shirt away a little, allowing his fingers to follow the line of my neck to my shoulder. I yank away from him, growling.

"Wait… you didn't have tattoos before." Helios's voice betrays his concern. I yank away from him again, pulling the shirt up to cover my shoulder.

I know what he's talking about. Occasionally, once I've fallen into the abyss, the makings for the pathway to the nightmares temporarily etch onto my skin. It might be gone by the morning, or it might be there for a few days, but there isn't usually this much of a delay before it appears. I know it's because of Helios, but I am not going to tell him that.

"Something is happening. Something more than what you have said. Isn't it?" Helios asks.

Yes. You are helping me and destroying me all at the same time. Dreamwalking is taking more of a toll on me than anyone knows.

But I can't say any of that, so instead, I say, "I'm trying to sleep. Stop talking."

Helios does not withdraw his hand. Instead, he glides his fingers down my arm and over my shirt. My skin burns from the contact. I bat his hand away, swatting at him. "You didn't want to touch me."

I'm not sure where that came from. This is one of the worst parts of having a mind like mine. It is so fucking difficult to separate my own thoughts from the others crowding my mind, but the second the statement leaves my lips, the thought is there. He'd barely touched me on the shoulder. He'd barely even looked at me. Why am I so annoyed by that?

"What?" Helios growls. "What are you talking about?"

"Sleeping." However, the snarl is not indicative of that.

Helios grabs my hip. "Are you saying I didn't want to touch you?"

I don't reply, just lying there with my eyes closed, seething over something ridiculous.

He pulls me onto my back, cupping my face. "Are you talking about the shower?"

I look up at him, my eyes hard. "I'm sleeping, Helios."

He squeezes my jaw, forcing me to keep my eyes on his. "I wanted to, but I know I've pushed your goodwill far today."

I smack his hand away. "Whatever." I am such a petulant asshole.

Helios slams his lips to mine, kissing me deeply, passionately, taking my breath away. He bites my lip, tugging it with him as he pulls back. My lip throbs as it slides from his teeth, already swelling up.

"Shh, go to sleep, kitten."

Oh, that little fucker.

"Fuck you."

He smirks down at me. "You're making me blush with all of this flirting."

I shove him off me and roll onto my side again, giving him my back, but I feel my lips curve into a smile. He sinks his teeth into my shoulder before settling beside me, and I relax easily into sleep.

LICKING MY FINGER, I TURN THE PAGE WITH FLOURISH, watching Melinoë out of the corner of my eye. I doubt she'll last long before her curiosity gets the best of her. I make sure the next page flip is even louder, the paper sliding noisily across the one beneath it. Out of the corner of my eye, I see her muscles shiver with irritation.

She holds out longer than I expect her to but finally snaps, "What are you reading?"

I loudly flip the page. "The History of Concrete."

She lets out a sound of actual distress. "You can't seriously be this boring."

I laugh at the way her face contorts with legitimate fear at the idea that she could be in a relationship with someone who casually reads about concrete. "It's fascinating to me how things get recorded, especially since we're both older than its invention."

She recoils, her face contorting even more. "Speak for yourself, Grandpa. I'm vibrant and youthful." She rolls onto her side, her back to me. "Just cause you're frail and wrinkly."

Fuck, I love sparring with her. Every verbal volley gets me hard. Her insults and threats of violence are even more delicious. I flip the page loudly again. "Sleep, my vibrant, youthful girlfriend."

She's pinned me beneath her in a blink, just like I knew she would. "Call me your girlfriend again, and I'll chop your dick off."

I moan, deliberately rolling my eyes to provoke her even

more. "Don't flirt with me."

She grabs my book and tosses it against the wall. It hits hard enough that it explodes the binding, sending the pages flying. "Fucking weirdo."

"Hey!"

She flips me off before rolling off me, giving me her back again. I glance at the mess she's made, papers littering the floor, and shrug. She shuffles on the bed, trying to get comfortable. I shift closer to her and warm my body again, luring her closer.

She growls without looking at me. "Back off, you walking melanoma."

I ignore her and pull her against my side, slowly changing my body temperature, increasing it to make it comfortable. She elbows me hard, and I hiss. "Just… It helps you sleep."

She's quiet for a long moment, and I'm not sure what she's going to do. This is the thing that I find so fascinating and alluring about her. She is so predictable yet so unpredictable at the same time. How could anyone not be entranced by her? Not want to understand, yet never understand, to always be surprised?

"I won't tell anyone," I whisper. This is the crux of everything. She is so afraid to admit weakness to anyone, but most of all, to herself.

It is another long moment before she rolls to face me. Her eyes lock on mine, trying to decipher and understand me. Am I just as much a puzzle to her as she is to me?

She moves a little closer to me and brushes her lips against mine. The touch is so soft it barely feels like a kiss, more like a butterfly brushing against the petals of a flower. Or a dagger along a throat. It's not enough.

I dig my fingers into her hair, gripping it tight, close to tearing it from the roots as she presses her body against mine. Her tongue darts between my lips, dancing with mine, not dueling or dominating, but almost playing with it. Her knee rises along my leg to rest at my hip, my fingers disentangling from her hair to trace along her skin. She feels so cold against my fingers, especially when I've warmed my body to such a degree.

I tighten my fingers on her knee and pull until she's straddling me again, but there's something different about this time, just like there was something different between us in the shower. There is a heaviness to our breath and meaning to our touch, a vulnerability we are sharing that neither of us wants to address.

Melinoë drags her nails across my shoulders but doesn't break the skin. She pulls away and kisses down my chest, and I have to bite back a moan. She's not… She is. I doubt she realizes she's never done this for me with no strings.

This is… a couple thing, offering pleasure without expectations because you simply can't resist. I don't dare speak as she slides lower, curling her fingers into my sweats and tugging them down. I barely muffle a groan at the way her eyes follow my bobbing cock, but I can't stop the sounds that come from my throat when she licks the sensitive tip. She takes me deeper into her mouth, painfully slowly, torturously slow.

Nevermind. I was wrong. This is definitely not pleasure without expectations. This is actual torture. I lift my hips toward her head, trying to get more of my cock into her mouth. She moves with me and shifts back but doesn't release me.

"Take more," I hiss.

Her eyes sparkle up at me as she waves her hand. My wrists are yanked over my head, held there by her nightmares. I tug hard against them, but the disembodied hands only tighten.

She smirks and slides her plump lips up my shaft, letting them catch on the flared head.

"Baby…" I whimper. Fuck it, I'm not above begging at this point, but it looks like Melinoë is settling in to torment me. She takes her mouth off me completely before dragging her teeth along the side of my shaft, and I twist my body, just trying to get more of her. "What do I have to do to get you to suck my cock?" I demand, desperation making me contort my body, trying to get out of the hold her hands have on me. I moan as she darts her tongue through my slit.

"Beg," she orders, her voice curling around me like her nightmare tendrils.

Does she think I won't? That I'm above begging? Has she not been paying attention?

"Baby… please suck my cock," I groan, my hands fisting, the muscles in my forearms bulging. At this point, I will beg for anything from her, so long as she keeps touching me, tasting me. She drags her nails down my thighs, licking the underside of my shaft. I can feel the way my cock jolts at the touch.

"You'll have to do better than that," she purrs, continuing the maddening flicks of her tongue. Each lick feels closer to a whip on my sensitive skin. My breath catches, and my cock twitches again at the idea of her using a whip on my cock.

Another time… Right now, I need to figure out what she wants, and how to beg better because I need this.

I pant and look down at her. Her pupils have absorbed her dual-colored eyes. "Please suck my cock and sit on my face when you do." She dips her head and sucks one of my balls into the wet heat of her mouth, rolling her tongue around it. I jolt, my eyes rolling back. "Fuck, please!"

Melinoë releases the sensitive flesh and blows a stream of cool air over it. "You've not earned my pussy," she says before swiping her tongue over my other ball and taking it into the heat of her mouth, leaving my cock feeling like it's about to burst.

Fuck.

I wrap my legs around her torso, trying to tug her to me. Maybe she'll listen to reason if I can get her to sit on my face. She moans and slides her tongue along my shaft as more of those nightmare hands appear from beneath the bed and pull my ankles down, binding them to the bed. I struggle against the hold, but she sucks my tip into her mouth, and all thought fades from my mind. I let out a whimper and lift my hips, trying to get deeper.

She slams her head down on me suddenly, taking my cock completely down her throat, all the way to the hilt. My eyes roll back, and pleasure shoots through me, my mind barely able to understand the overwhelming sensation. She swallows around me, and I tremble, everything amplified. My body twists and turns, searching for relief but finding none. She releases my cock with her lips and fists me, slowly stroking my shaft.

"More," I moan.

She tightens her grip before taking me back into the wet heat of her mouth and sucking hard. Her tongue curls around my shaft, sliding along the underside of my cock with each pull. My toes curl, and I swear I see the secrets of the universe.

"I'm already close," I pant, writhing.

Her lips form a seal, taking me down her throat over and over. My eyes roll back, and my hips buck helplessly, shooting my cum down her throat, the release making my body arch with relief and pleasure. She swallows me down, sucking my sensitive tip, licking me clean before she looks up at me. I pant, my body sapped of energy and cum.

She waves her hand to release me and turns on her side.

Her back to me.

"I'm sleeping now," she says.

I ignore her and pull her against me. "I know."

My body is still trembling, and I'm not sure how long it takes to get my sanity back, but by the time I do, she's already fast asleep.[8]

---

[8] The Queen & The King Chapter 15

Chapter Sixteen

IN THE PAST, IT WAS ALWAYS STRANGE NOT TO SLEEP WHEN OTHERS DID. Even after forfeiting some of my powers, sleep is still a foreign concept to me. It never used to fascinate me before, but when Melinoë rests next to me, I am transfixed. Her face is soft with sleep, none of the feigned expressions she uses to pretend disgust toward me or disdain for others—two of her favorite tools to divert attention from her craving for acceptance.

Fuck, I'm still reeling from that blowjob. What was that about? She just gave without any expectation of me returning the favor. It was different for her.

Melinoë cuddles closer, and as the minutes turn to hours, she ends up on top of me. She scratches at her nose clumsily, bringing a smile to my face as I scratch it for her. An hour later, she laughs softly in her sleep before burying her face against my neck.

I stroke a hand down her back. "That's right. I'll keep the darkness away."

My phone pings with a message.

S

Spoke to him, he's not even willing to consider another side.

I sigh. Of course, Selene went off to speak with our father without me. She's so fucking stubborn sometimes.

Despite Eos and Selene wanting me to pick a side, they went off and made it even harder for me to choose one.

H

I told you I'd do things myself, in my own way.

I squeeze the phone in my hands, making Melinoë shift slightly on my chest. My body warms, lulling her back to sleep before I can formulate a reply.

H

She doesn't have anything to do with this.

That might be the biggest lie I've ever told. There is little I do these days that doesn't have something to do with her.

S

If it wasn't for her, you'd already have made up your mind.

I growl softly, and Melinoë shifts on me. I wince and force myself to relax, waiting for her to drift off again.

H

I'm not interested in another thousand years in prison, so no, I would not have. You wanted me to make the choice, so let me fucking make it and back the fuck off.

Okay, that was pretty harsh, I guess. She is still my twin.

> **H**
>
> Sorry.

No reply. I suppose I deserve that. She'll cold-shoulder me for a while as a result. Selene is very two-faced, no doubt reflecting her celestial counterpart. The dark side of the moon is a frozen wasteland, after all. I pull up my chat with Eos and type out a message, but another one pops in before I can press send.

> **A**
>
> Dad's looking for you.

Every muscle in my body immediately locks down. I don't know what's more surprising: who the text is from or what the text actually says.

> **H**
>
> Actively?

Melinoë's brows furrow, and I exhale, my body slowly relaxing again. I stroke her hair. "I'll keep the darkness away." Using a muted light, I press my palm to the side of her head, dispelling some of the darkness in her dreams. She makes a contented sound before nuzzling deeper into my neck.

> **A**
>
> Not yet, planning on it, though.

Fuck that means I need to make a choice sooner rather than later. I sigh softly, looking at Melinoë asleep on my chest. How much more time do I have before the end begins? Before I have to make a choice that might end with me betraying my family, my people, or her?

She shifts suddenly, putting her pussy right on top of my cock, and the greedy fucker immediately reacts. Fuck, she's so wet. She rocks against me, responding to me even in sleep. I can think about picking sides another time. Right now, I want her to wake up riding my cock. I hold her hips and slowly press my cock inside her, waiting to see if she wakes up. She moans and flexes her hips but remains asleep. Yet she gets wetter, drenching my cock, squeezing me.

"Helios…" she whimpers, her lips brushing my neck.

I know she thinks this is a dream, and I buck my hips, making her bounce, purposely waking her.

Her nails dig in, and her eyes slowly blink open. "Helios?"

I grab her hips tight, knowing I am adding bruises to her perfect skin, and force her down on me harder. She cries out and arches, her dual-colored eyes locking with mine. They are still misty with sleep but slowly becoming more and more focused on me. I roll us to put her beneath me and grab her wrists in a single hand, pulling them above her head. I brace myself on one arm and thrust into her deeper and faster.

"You got your control last night," I rasp. "Now, it's my turn."

Her eyes go clear, sharp, and aware, all sleep gone. A naked vulnerability lurks in the depth of her gaze, one that she has not yet had the time to cover. Right now, her walls are down. I lean down to press my lips to hers, tasting her and her darkness edged with insanity. The darkness I've never known yet long to explore with her.

If you lose yourself to your darkness, take me with you. I would rather live in madness with you than in sanity with anyone else.

She melts beneath my lips, and I am humbled by her trust in me. I tighten my hold on her wrists, bruising her with my handprint, making her surrender. She writhes beneath me like she is in the throes of her madness. The struggle only makes my cock ache even more, and I fuck her harder. Her teeth sink into my lower lip, breaking the skin, my blood flavoring our kiss. I bite her lip in turn, mixing our ichor. I wrap my free hand around her throat and squeeze.

"You want to come, baby?" I groan against her lips. She wraps her legs around my hips, her heels digging into my ass. I tighten my fingers on her slender neck when she doesn't respond. "Say it."

She meets my next thrust, taking me deeper and grinding against me. "Want to come—"

I cut off her air completely, and her cunt squeezes me. She lets out a strangled scream as she comes, her body demanding I follow. Even when I am supposedly the one in charge, my body is her slave. I release her throat and then her hands. Our breaths mingle, our lips still stained in each other's blood.

"Morning," I drawl, unable to hold back my smirk.

She presses her lip to mine, no doubt still feeling the same euphoria I do. But the moment shatters around us, and she breaks the kiss, shoving me off her. I'm too surprised by the shift to fight her about it. She lunges out of bed and grabs one of my shirts, yanking it and her boots on. Every movement is jerky and unnatural. It's the same way she moved when lost in her head, yet her eyes are clear.

"Baby," I cajole. "Where are you going?"

Is she feeling exposed and vulnerable? Like I am?

"I ate. I slept," she states, precisely and emotionlessly. "Remove the cuff."

I don't know why, but this hurts. I am used to brushing off Melinoë's words. They're foreplay for us, lies she says but doesn't truly believe. It's a game between us, but at this moment, there is nothing fun about it. No, right now, her eyes are not guarded, and they're not sparkling with her madness. They're cold.

I'd forgotten. How could I forget?

Darkness is not the only thing I've never experienced. I stand, waving my hand so the adamantium around her ankle snaps open and drops to the bedroom floor. I want to say something. I usually have a ready response or a flirtatious comment, but right now, I have nothing.

Melinoë grabs one of my belts and cinches it at the waist. "Later."

"Right," I squeeze through my clogged throat. "Later."

I turn away, not wanting to actually see her shadow away from me. I can't handle it right now. Not until I figure out exactly what's wrong with me and why I'm suddenly feeling so... exposed right now. But Melinoë never does what I expect.

Instead of leaving me without another word, she closes the distance and turns me back around. She kisses me. It's not a long or even a passionate kiss, but it's everything to me at that moment. Even when she pulls away with a frown and vanishes without another word, that momentary lapse was hope for me.

Chapter Seventeen

Helios

IT IS HARD TO NOT FOLLOW HER. Everything in me screams not to let her go, to keep her close. But I made a promise, and foolishly, I want her to come to me this time. I don't know why I think she will. She's a stubborn little thing, but it doesn't stop me from wanting it. Isn't that always what happens? We want things we know will never happen. We hold on to cheap fortunes from cookies, wish on stars shooting across the sky, and toss coins into a well. And I, the fool I am, hope this girl will come to me for the first time.

Melinoë claims she's going on a date, but I refuse to believe it means anything. If it meant something, she wouldn't have told me in hopes I would interfere. Glancing at my phone, I'm tempted to pick it up, to call any of the contacts there who I could take out. The only problem is the one I want to take out on a date is the one leaving right now.

Fuck, I need to get out of the house. This is pathetic. I'm becoming the type of person I hate. I grab the first set of clothes I see. Thankfully, they all pass the sniff test. The second I'm on the street, I have no fucking idea where I should go. I suppose it is New York. There is no shortage of things to do. Yet, I find myself just wandering. I've lived in a lot of places all over the world in the last thousand years, but New York is probably the loudest. The towering skyscrapers block the dimming rays of the sun, and the sharp fall air has the people of the city bundling up as they travel to and from work.

I enjoy New York, but I'm not sure I would truly call it home. I'm not sure if I've ever had a place to truly call home. It is somewhat of a foreign concept to me. Olympus wasn't really a comforting place, even when Titans ruled.

"Helios," a voice calls, drifting to me on the air, crisp and cool, my entire body snapping straight.

My feet plant on the sidewalk, my muscles locking down. "I would think a Titaness of Sight would know I have no interest in speaking to her."

I glance over my shoulder, locking eyes with the lurking goddess. She smiles and moves from the shadows, linking her arm with mine and forcing me to continue walking. "Don't cause a scene. We have eyes on us."

With her hold on me, I walk down the street, though it feels more like a hostage situation. "You could have called, Mother."

I toss the title out like an insult, which, to me, it is. She might have given birth to my sisters and me, but there was a moment when she surrendered all rights to call herself my mother.

"Would you have answered?" she asks smoothly, holding my arm tightly.

"I told you what would happen when you chose," I hiss back through a forced smile. She chose this moment on purpose. She chose every moment on purpose. Theia, the Titaness of Sight, knew what was coming far before many people even made the decision that would lead them on such a path. So she knew the exact results that would occur when she chose all those years ago, and she still chose him.

"He's my husband. He needed me," she responds, her tone barely changing. It's as if we are discussing the weather rather than the prominent divide between mother and son.

"We were your children. We needed you." I yank my arm from her grasp, not caring if we draw a scene. The eyes on us don't matter.

"He's planning to unleash the Father of Monsters," she whispers, her voice lost in the bustle around us for a moment.

I freeze again. Theia could be lying. She is good at that, too good. "He didn't do that last time."

However, he had debated it. Unease spears through me. Desperation made sane men dangerous. I cannot imagine what desperation would turn the King of the Titans into.

"Things are different this time," she says, and I turn to face her. Theia's expression is cut with seriousness, her dark hair shining in the low light. Her coloring is another stark difference between my mother and us. Even our father shares no physical similarities with my sisters and me.

My eyes scan hers, trying to read the future in them, but nothing even hints at what she's seen. "You've made your choice. Again." That, I can see in her eyes.

She nods.

"You won't influence me one way or another," I say, even as she closes the distance between us and puts her hand on my arm. "I will choose based on what will keep my sisters and me safe."

She leans up and kisses my cheek. "I know, Helios."

This time, I don't pull away. Instead, I close my eyes and lean into her slightly. I know she will never pick us over my father. She will always choose him, no matter how perfect we are, how hard we work, and how much affection we give her. A child should never have to prove to their parents that they are worthy of love.

"Goodbye, Mother," I whisper, knowing she'll be gone when I open my eyes again. She'd delivered her message to me and would not spend a second longer in my presence.

Though she's not the only female in my life with that particular predilection, the difference between her and Melinoë is that I actually want one of them around.

I immediately turn back toward my apartment. Why did I even leave in the first place? There is nothing pathetic about waiting around for the woman I love. That's some toxic ass shit to believe. My steps are lighter as I make my way back to my flat. She will be back. I know it.

Chapter Eighteen
Melinoë

TWENTY-EIGHT HOURS, THREE MINUTES AND ELEVEN SECONDS. That's how long it's been since I last saw or heard from Helios, and they have been fucking bliss. In fact, they have been so perfect that I have barely even thought of him. Because why would I? I hate him and his stupid golden face.

I sit in my office at Plutus Industries, tapping a pen against the desk and glancing at my phone for maybe the eightieth time in the past five minutes. Nothing. I thought he would message me the second we reached the end of my freedom, yet the clock on my phone reluctantly counts through the minutes without a word from him. Time seems to have slowed since 2:18 PM. That was the precise time that our agreed-upon separation was supposed to end. But as I watch the time on my phone sluggishly drag on to 2:24 PM, I feel the restlessness in my bones.

The voices have gotten progressively louder, and I've been trying to push them back. I want to prove to both of us I am in control of my own mind and that I don't need him. I'm a delusional asshole, but my delusion is my savior.

I haven't been to Plutus Industries in weeks. Luckily, I'm best friends with the boss's wife. Officially, I didn't have to work. Hades had offered me the same deal he had offered to all the gods who had left Olympus looking for more. Despite growing up feral, lost, and alone, he had allowed me to stay in the mortal world, even though I am more unpredictable than your average Olympian. However, he had added one stipulation. I understood it, even if I'd always had better manners than that fucker, Zeus.

We agreed I would get the same allowance as the other Olympians, but Hades would monitor me more closely. He found me my apartment, and I was to check in with him via text at least once a day, in person at least once a week. He had one rule, and if I ever broke it, he would send me back to the Underworld. I was never to lay a harmful finger on a human. He assured me the consequences would be severe if I did, but nothing could be as bad as my reality before he saved me.

One day, I showed up at his office for our weekly check-in, and I think he could see in my eyes that I was still painfully lost. He'd offered me a job, and having that purpose was the greatest feeling. That is until I met Persephone. She was my first true friend. I suppose Hades was my friend, but it's difficult to have an easy friendship with someone to whom you owe your entire life. Well, that and the fact that he was obnoxiously dull before P came into his life.

My co-workers had gone silent when I stepped through the elevator doors and into the familiar basement of Plutus Industries this morning. The decor down here is infinitely more muted than that of the other departments. My boots had been loud even against the dark green carpet as I walked across the bullpen to my office. At least twenty sets of eyes burned into me, their intrigue like an itchy Christmas sweater. Before I stepped into my office, I whirled on my heel, casting a devilish gaze over each one of my observers, pulling my lips into a wicked smile. They all squirreled away, diverting their gazes so fast I bet they gave themselves eyeball whiplash.

My lips twitch at the memory, but it vanishes in an instant when my phone lights up. I snatch it up embarrassingly quick and swipe across my lock screen picture of an animated black cat wearing a Mike Myers mask and holding a bloody machete. There is an email notification reminding me that my subscription renewal for Verra's Interior Design for the Halloween Inclined is coming up soon.

The time seems to jump out at me, and I narrow my eyes, seeing that it is now 2:29 PM. Eleven minutes since he could have reached out. Could he have finally realized that I'm completely batshit? Does he now see the depths of my disinterest?

I open my desk drawer and throw my phone inside, snarling as I slam it closed. Turning my attention back to my computer, I select one of the unanswered IT tickets, but before I even read through the query, someone is knocking on my door. I look up, anticipating the feeling of thick, sweet honey at the back of my throat, but it never comes. I narrow my eyes. "What?" I snap, my mood irate after being alone for so many hours, something I used to be exceptionally good at.

A head with dark brown hair pops around the door, and I'm greeted with a boyish smile. Human. Gross. He enters after a moment, obviously realizing that he's not going to get anything other than an indignant stare from me. He's maybe in his mid to late twenties, tall, pale, and skinny, his nose covered in a smattering of freckles. Even though he stands at around 5'10, Helios would dwarf him.

"Hi!" he says, his voice sure, but there's an undercurrent of nerves that the average person wouldn't detect.

"Yeah?" I ask impatiently. I can practically hear Helios's response in my mind. He'd probably get hard at the snipe. Weirdo.

The nervous human's heart rate speeds up, his pulse fluttering in his neck as fast as the wings of a hovering hummingbird.

"Uh, hi? Usually, that's how we greet someone?" he stammers out.

I lift my chin, narrowing my eyes, studying him. What a strange creature. Doesn't he have any survival instincts?

He smiles kindly at me. "I'm Michael. I'm new."

"Obviously."

"Well, I was…" He pauses for a moment, seeming to psych himself up. "I was wondering if you wanted to go out tonight?"

"Go out?" I repeat, blinking.

"With me, on a date."

A date? With a human? A human who definitely isn't my type?

"Why?" I ask, perplexed. Surely, I can't be his type, either. He looks like he would go rock solid for the girl next door, happy to keep her barefoot and pregnant.

I shudder at the thought of such a person, such a couple. At least Helios likes the same sort of stuff I do, even if he does have the sun shining out of his ass. Although I also hate Helios and want him to leave me alone forever.

I feel the human's eyes on me, looking at me expectantly.

"Well?" I prompt, annoyed at waiting for him to answer.

"Oh, I said… because I like you."

I glance at the drawer housing the physical manifestation of Helios ignoring me. I roll my eyes and stand. "What am I? A beacon for weird stalkers?" I start to pace, longing for the pacing area in my apartment, with the worn track marks and the comforting color fade. I yank my drawer open and grab my phone. Opening my text thread with Persephone, I type out a message.

MELLIE

> P, I don't know what's wrong with me. I've had glorious space from my carcinogenic stalker but I'm still thinking about his dumb face. Do you think he drugged me with the food from the other day? Or do you think there was something funky about that cuff? Fucking Helios. Also I've just been asked out by this weird human from Plutus and he's so...odd. How did you do it with Jackson for so long (RIP).

Just getting the words out makes me feel ten tons lighter. The human clears his throat, and my head snaps up. Gods. Didn't he leave already?

"So is that a no?" he asks.

I glance at my phone, my gaze snagging on my text chain with Helios, and my blood boils. "Eight pm, the movie theater down the street," I practically snarl.

"Really?" The hopefulness in his voice genuinely makes me feel nauseous.

"I'm about to change my mind," I growl at him.

"Okay! Eight!" He grins and scurries away.

I slump back down into my desk chair. 2:45 PM. My phone finally pings, and my whole body seems to know exactly who it is. My skin tingles in anticipation and annoyance at the message I haven't even read yet from my six-foot-four walking sunspot.

HELIOS

Are you busy tonight?

The message is so simple it surprises me. I'm not sure what I expected. Maybe a disgustingly emotional sonnet about how deeply he's missed me. Maybe a few dirty lines about how desperately he needs me. But no, just a simple question. One that doesn't even prompt more of an answer than one word. I glare at the message, willing it to be more. I snarl at my phone, shoving it back in my drawer and slamming it closed again.

I manage to finish the full workday and make my way home before I look at it again. My phone feels like a lead weight in my pocket, and the voices whisper in favor of reading the message, making it easier to drag me into the darkness. The smarter voices warn against it, knowing that single question is enough to lead me back to him. They are muted to less than a hushed whisper in his presence, and they want to avoid that.

I sit on my couch and stare at my phone. The black screen taunts me, and the longer I look at it, the more I swear I can see it lightly vibrating. The unanswered message calls to me like a songbird calls to the morning.

I stab aggressively at my phone, waking it up. The message is already open, the cursor flashing aggressively at me, awaiting my words.

MELLIE

Yes.

I know my response is pathetic, but it's truthful and all his stupid initial message deserves.

Butterflies start the most intense mosh pit in my stomach as I watch the three dots stupidly bounce up and down as he types.

HELIOS

Doing what?

MELLIE

I have a date.

The honest response tastes like acid, but I need to put some distance between us. I think.

HELIOS

No you don't.

His response burrows under my skin uncomfortably, and suddenly, the moshing butterflies burst into flames, the fluttering inferno fueling my anger. I lock my phone and chuck it down on the couch, deciding to get ready for my date. I've barely made it to my closet when I hear the heavy sound of Helios's hand against my door, dragging my attention from the array of black fabric in front of me.

"Melinoë!" he snarls, knocking on my front door so hard I think he probably has a pretty good shot at breaking it down.

I change into a short, black t-shirt dress and fishnet tights with my purple Dr. Martens before slowly applying my makeup. Helios's growling, snarling, and punching is the perfect "getting-ready" playlist for my night.

He doesn't let up, not for a single second, but I don't go to him until I've finished sweeping my deep purple lipstick over my lips, blending the color with the black liner I used.

"Melinoë! Let me in, now!" he snarls.

I roll my eyes and make my way to the door, wrenching it open. Helios's fist pauses midair, his dark, furious eyes sweeping over me.

His skin is dull, duller than I've ever seen it, and his face looks drawn. He looks tired, which is ridiculous because Helios doesn't sleep.

His frown deepens. "You're wearing makeup?" he states, though it sounds like a question.

I glare at him. "I'm not interested in buying any encyclopedias. Thanks, though," I say and try to push the doors closed, but Helios grabs my arm, his large body shoving the door back, the room shaking with the force of it hitting the wall.

"Where are you going?"

I yank my arm away, pushing as much venom in my glare as possible.

"You're not going on an actual date," he growls.

I cross my arms over my chest, lifting my chin as I scowl at him. "What do you want, Helios?"

He moves in closer, crowding me. "I wanted to see you. I…" He hesitates and looks down at me. His gaze captures mine, holding it captive. "I missed you."

My brows draw together, and his stare becomes more intense as he searches my eyes, though I'm not sure what he's looking for. The butterflies in my stomach rise from the ashes and are once again slamming against each other.

Helios tilts his head slightly and leans in, my pulse hammering in my neck, my heart slamming as our breath mingles. His lips are velvet soft as he brushes them against mine, but his whole body tenses when my phone alerts, cutting through the silence of the room like a serrated blade. He slides his tongue along the seam of my lips, asking for permission. I grant him access, and the second his tongue brushes against mine, I moan, pressing my body to his.

My phone alerts again, and Helios slides his hands over my waist to cup my ass, moving them beneath my dress, the pads of his fingers trailing scorching heat over my skin. I pull back to check my phone, and when I see the message from the mortal, it's like I've been dunked into a bucket of ice-cold water.

Helios just slides his lips to my neck, trailing searing hot kisses down my shoulder. "Melinoë," he moans, and the sound nearly sends me to my knees.

My gaze snags on my phone again, and I tug myself away from him. "I'm late."

Helios frowns, my lipstick smudging his lips. "You're seriously going on a date?" he asks, watching me with the beginnings of what looks like pain in his eyes.

"Why wouldn't I?"

"You know exactly why," he growls, baring his teeth

slightly.

I glance at his lips once more before turning and leaving my apartment. I feel him hot on my heels. "So, I should go on a date too?" he asks, the anger stark in his voice.

I shrug. "Whatever."

I hear him stop and then storm away in the other direction. I swallow down the acidic taste of my lie and lift my chin, fixing my makeup in a small compact mirror I borrowed from Persephone as I go.

As I walk to the movie theater, I try my best to force all thoughts of Helios out of my mind. Maybe I'll like hanging out with a mortal. Persephone didn't hate Jackson until her mother switched him out. She also never committed to him and given her boner for committing to Hades, who is boring as fuck, I don't have high hopes for anyone from the mortal race entertaining me.

I walk past countless humans, all of whom are wearing boring, shapeless winter wear. Fuck. Do I even remember what this guy looks like? I think he had hair and maybe a nose.

"Hey!" His freckled face invades my vision, and I blink. "Ready for the movie?"

"Sure, whatever," I say, and he hands me a small paper ticket with the name of some newly released horror movie. I appreciate the effort. He obviously thinks he knows me and that this is my vibe. It probably looks like it is the kind of movie I would enjoy, but honestly, there is a documentary about porpoises playing, which I would definitely have preferred.

Helios would have known that.

The human holds out his hand as if waiting for me to slide mine into it, and my hand literally burns from the idea of placing it against another's skin.

I laugh, crossing my arms. "Absolutely not."

He looks kind of rejected, and I feel guilt claw beneath my skin.

This motherfucking conscience is fucking annoying.

"I'm not a hand-holding kind of girl," I add, and he seems to brighten up a little.

"Oh, okay." Michael leads me to the concessions counter, the smell of butter and burnt popcorn filling the air. "Are you a snack kind of girl?" he quips, glancing at me, amusement dancing in his eyes.

I nod and browse the selection. Without thinking, I grab a bag that I'm drawn to.

"Chocolate-covered pretzels? Good choice!" Michael

says, looking at my selection.

I blink down at the bag, dread clenching my intestines. Helios's favorite. How the fuck do I know that? I grab a bag of gummy worms but keep hold of the pretzels. Michael pays before leading me into theater number eight, where the slasher movie will start in the next ten minutes.

The human climbs the stairs, going right to the back of the theater and selecting two seats roughly in the middle. I'm not naïve. I know these are the make-out seats, and I eye him suspiciously. He's been the perfect gentleman until now, but if he thinks he can cop a feel when the lights dim, he'll be leaving with a few more broken bones than he came in with.

I look down at the bag of pretzels, frowning. My lips still tingle from the warmth of Helios's. The lights go down, and sound from the speakers boom from all around us as the trailers begin. Michael takes the bag of pretzels and opens them, eating one. I snatch them instinctively, needing to protect them.

Michael blinks at me. "What?"

I hand him the bag of gummy worms. "These are better."

"I can't have pretzels?" he asks, bewildered. His voice is quiet compared to the trailer for another upcoming horror movie.

"No. They've gone bad." I look at the screen, clutching the bag of pretzels tight and drawing my knees up, wrapping my arms around them.

The movie has barely begun when I feel the human's arm snaking around my shoulders. I hiss at him.

"Are you okay?" he asks, watching me warily.

"You know, I actually have to go," I say. I stand, still holding tight to the bag of pretzels.

"But the movie just—"

"Absolutely! It was great!" I stuff a ten-dollar bill into the collar of his shirt. "For the pretzels. See ya!"

I can't get out of there fast enough. The second he took the bag of pretzels from me and ate one, I knew I needed to leave.

It doesn't even surprise me when I arrive at Helios's apartment. I think I accepted that this was where I needed to be on my distracted walk from the most boring date I've ever been on. I don't even knock on his door, using my shadows to shatter the lock from inside before stepping in.

His scent immediately envelopes me, and I practically groan at the feeling of it. I walk into his living room, not even questioning why he's lying on the floor, staring up at the ceiling. Sometimes, I do that, too.

I drop the bag of pretzels on the floor next to him, a few spilling out onto the rug. He frowns, looking at the small chocolate-covered savory twists, then up at me.

"Not one fucking word," I warn. My tone and body language may be threatening and tense, but I feel as if I take my first real breath in 34 hours, 24 minutes, and 36 seconds.

Chapter Nineteen

Helios

I DIDN'T HAVE TO WAIT LONG FOR HER TO COME BACK AFTER HER DATE. She breaks my lock and throws open the door of my flat, dropping a bag of chocolate-covered pretzels onto my chest.

Melinoë starts undressing on her way to the bedroom, and I follow like a lovesick swain, which I unashamedly am. Within forty-five minutes, we're in a tangle of limbs, a discarded knife that's only a little bloody on the bed next to us. Panting, I kiss her, a sheen of sweat lingering on my skin.

"I'm happy you came."

She pulls back slightly. "You're so average in bed. I almost didn't."

Says the woman who just came on my cock while I held a knife to her throat.

"Thanks." I smirk, a laugh bubbling in my throat. "I try."

She glares at me, but her eyes sparkle with humor. I toss the knife into the wall, letting it embed itself there before leaning in and kissing her deeply. She shadows away mid-kiss, and I fall off the side of the bed, landing face-first on the ground. I groan and hoist myself up on my arms, scrunching my nose to see if it is bruised or broken. The movement doesn't bring tears to my eyes. Bruised.

I jump to my feet, prepared to begin the chase for Melinoë, but the sound of my television turning on in the living room stops me. Pulling the blanket around my shoulders, I walk into the living room, and sure enough, Melinoë is sitting naked on my couch, flicking through the channels. I silently sit beside her and extend my arm, inviting her close and offering part of the blanket.

She doesn't look at me as she shifts closer and curls against my side. She presses into me. "Don't get used to this, dumbass."

I smother a smile and kiss the top of her head. "Wouldn't dream of it, hellcat." She wiggles out of my arms and leans down to grab the bag of pretzels she'd tossed at me the night before. "Mmm, my favorite," I say, taking the bag and popping one into my mouth.

My skin glows as she curls back against me. I chew contentedly as she lands on another home reconstruction show. "Do you mind? You're causing a glare," she growls grumpily.

In all honesty, I can control the glow of my skin, but I like wearing my heart on my literal sleeve for Melinoë. So, instead, I grab a pair of sunglasses off the side table and hold them out to her.

She rolls her eyes. "You're a moron."

I chuckle, and she slaps my chest. We watch the show in silence, but she clearly wants to say something. I think she is hoping I will bring it up first, but she'll be waiting a long time as mind reading is decidedly not one of my powers.

"So…" she begins, pulling at one of her fingers. "Did you… go on a date?"

I keep myself from tensing, but just barely. "No. Did you?"

She went on a date. There was no other reason for her to ask me that. My rational side reminds me that she came to me, like I hoped she would, despite going out on a date with another person. However, the irrational side of me is thinking of all the ways to find the person and turn them into a charred corpse.

"Yes," she drawls. "We went to the movies, hit it off, and now we're married, expecting our third child."

Just like that, the rational side wins out.

"Your body sure rebounds fast," I volley back.

"Sorry you weren't invited to the wedding. We were at capacity, and I knew your huge head wouldn't fit into the venue."

I love playing with her, especially like this. With every word, she's telling me how much she hated her date and wanted me instead.

"That makes sense. Plus, you were clearly concerned about calling it off the second you saw me." I smirk, biting her ear.

She hisses but doesn't move away. "I'd have called it off

because seeing your stupid face would have given me the ick for all men, including my husband."

"Or you'd sprint down the aisle and beg me to fuck you right there so your husband can take notes."

She tunnels her fingers into my hair, yanking my head to hers, hovering her lips over mine. "I hate you."

"Such a liar," I rumble against her lips. She's going to kiss me now, and we'll descend into the passion that simmers beneath our skin. Neither of us excels at keeping our hands off each other.

Instead of kissing me, she moves her hand to my neck, squeezing tightly. "You're not afraid of me. Ever."

She phrases it like a statement, but it's closer to a question. A question she is trying to understand. Her madness never frightens me. I've found there to be more truth in a moment of madness than a millennium of lies. I press my throat into her hand, giving her more control over me. Her eyes flash with insanity.

"Don't go where I can't follow," I whisper. "If you find yourself falling into your mind, don't leave me behind. Wherever you're going is where I am headed, too."

She shoves me back on the couch, holding me still by the throat. "Stop being a mushy weirdo."

I smirk, her hand loosening slightly. "Never."

Her lips twitch into a smile, and my skin glows brightly. "Stop glowing."

"No." I glow more deliberately.

Melinoë growls, the sound feral, and grabs my face. She kisses me hard, the taste of her laced with her brutal need and simmering insanity. Too soon, she pulls back, looking up at me. I stroke her cheek, staring into her mismatched eyes.

"I'm all yours," I assure her, silently asking her unspoken thoughts.

"Perfect," she rasps. "That means I can return you to the clingy dumbass store."

I laugh, leaning down to smother her in kisses. "But what if someone else purchases me?!"

Her face turns serious, and she wraps her legs around my waist, keeping me locked against her. "Then they're just as dumb as you are."

Emotion crawls up my throat, looking at her wrapped around me, threatening to break free. "I love you."

Chapter Twenty

Helios

MELINOË SHOVES ME OFF HER, AND I LAND ON MY BACK ON THE FLOOR. SMelinoë shoves me off her, and I land hard on the floor. She stands over me, glaring as I strain to breathe again. "What the fuck was that?" She demands, her hands on her hips.

I wince. Yeah, I hadn't meant to let that slip out already, but now that it was out, there was nothing I could really do about it. I can't unsay something, and this, I would not unsay even if I could rewind time.

"Take it back," she snarls.

I cough and stand up to face her. "No."

Melinoë narrows her eyes on me. I bite back a groan. She is so sexy, completely naked, the blanket discarded on the couch, and mad as hell. "If you ever say that shit to me again, I'll rip your spine out."

Okay, I was not expecting that level of vitriol at my confession. I suppose I should have been more prepared. It is Melinoë, after all. Yet, something lurks in her eyes, something she always tries to hide from me and herself. Fear.

"I love you," I repeat, my eyes locked on hers.

She shoves me hard and shadows away, taking me by surprise. Fuck, I should have seen that coming. I should have put the cuff back on her. I flash to grab clothes before I go to her apartment.

"Melinoë!" I shout, banging on the door.

A sign flashes on the door in her messy, scrawled script.

Helios Free Zone.

I rip the sign off, slamming my shoulder into the door.

It doesn't give even a little. Melinoë must have had it reinforced, and with how my shoulder is aching, she probably used some adamantium to do so.

"Open the fucking door!" I shout.

Fuck off.

"I will break it down!" The likelihood of me truly being able to do so is low, but she doesn't need to know that.

The door whips open. Melinoë stands there, wearing a silk robe with a burn mark on the thigh. I storm through the open door, though she tries to close it in my face. "Why did you run?"

She hits me, her hand bouncing off ineffectually. "Why did you say that?"

I grab her before she can run from me, wrapping my arms around her tightly. "Because it's true."

She hisses at me, her eyes sharp, but she doesn't fight me. I will count that as a victory. She doesn't pull away even as I lean down and kiss her.

"Hate you," she rasps against my lips.

"Liar."

I deepen the kiss, my fingers tunneling into her hair, keeping her locked against me. Her nails dig into my back, and she pulls me close.

"Does it scare you?" I murmur.

She presses her lips to mine again, her nails breaking the skin on my back, deepening her hold on me. "How much I hate you? Why would it?"

I bite her lip, pulling back to let it snap. "That I love you."

Her body stiffens, and she grabs me, shoving me back onto her couch. "Stop saying it."

"What?" I goad her. "That I love you?" Something is digging into my back. Not that I care when she straddles me.

"Stop."

Grabbing her hair, I yank her face to mine, locking my eyes on her mismatched ones. There's something more profound than fear lurking there, something worse than a nightmare to her. I thought it was simply fear at hearing how I feel, but it's more than that. It's an inability to understand a reality where someone can love her when she doesn't even love herself. That every demon in her head, every violent thought or action, every flaw and dent in her soul, only makes me love her more. She was a hurricane, and I don't want to clear the storm with the sun, not at all.

I want to dance in the rain.

"I love you," I repeat.

Melinoë tears out some of her hair when she rips away from me to stand. She yanks her shorts off, her panties following. "I said, shut the fuck up."

"I love you." I reach for her, trying to bring her back to me, but she bats my hands away and straddles my shoulders.

"Shut. The. Fuck. Up."

I groan, looking up at her cunt as she forces my silence with her soaking flesh. I bury my face against her, knowing one simple thing: she's in love with me, too.

Chapter Twenty-One
Melinoë

I LOVE YOU."

His words bounce around my mind, pinging along every neuron, filling every cell. Fuck, why did he have to say it?

"I love this pussy," he moans against me. His voice is muffled, but I still hear him.

I need him to stop talking. I grind my pussy against his mouth, his tongue sinfully circling my clit, setting my every nerve alight. I throw my head back, reveling in the insane, intense, and exquisite pleasure. Helios mumbles something into me, but I can't decipher it. He moans, sucking on my clit, and I arch, rocking my hips.

Helios pulls back a little, murmuring, "I love you." Again. I tunnel my fingers in his hair and yank hard, pushing his mouth back against my cunt. He stiffens his tongue, pushing it inside me, and I moan, losing myself to the pleasure. The declaration still trails over my skin, but it only adds to the pleasure. I don't want the words. I hate them, but why do they make me feel like I'm floating?

Helios bites my clit, and I cry out. The pain and pleasure melt together into the most exquisite bliss. He growls into me, sucking my clit once more, and I can't stop from falling over the edge of my orgasm. His name echoes around the room, torn from my lips by the pleasure he is forcing from me. My body tenses beneath the waves of ecstasy.

I roll off him and hit the floor hard, but I barely notice the dull ache in my spine. My chest heaves as I stare at the ceiling, coming down from my orgasm.

"You could have stayed on my face." I hear the smirk in Helios's voice, but I ignore him, lost in my thoughts.

He can't love me.

Helios follows me off the couch, landing on me but supporting his weight on his hands so he doesn't crush me. He eases his body down against mine, pressing close, his bright, glowing face taking up the space of the white ceiling I was previously enjoying staring at.

"Get off, you giant ball of radiating plasma," I say, but I make no move to push him off, his weight somehow comforting me.

He brushes his lips over mine. "Nope."

I sigh heavily, just glaring at him.

He leans down, whispering into my lips, "And you know what? Even though I can tell you are rejecting the words, I still love you. It's still true."

I growl, slapping him across the face.

He groans, the sound coming from low in his stomach. "Doesn't change anything."

"Cancerous fucker," I growl.

He smirks. "Your cancerous fucker." He presses his lips to mine, and I can't help but kiss him back. It is soft and tender, and I can only tolerate it for so long, pulling back after a moment. Helios's face turns serious as he looks down at me.

"Does it scare you?" he whispers, the question more loaded than any I've ever been asked.

Everything about Helios scares me, and that is fucking terrifying. I lived in the bowels of the Underworld for centuries, and I have faced countless nightmares and conjured even more. Yet, here I am, looking up at this glowing daydream, and I have never been more afraid. I think about what Hades and Persephone are going through, and my fears seem pathetic.

"I'm not scared of anything," I say because lying is so much less complex than the truth. A truth I'm not ready to explore myself, never mind let someone else explore with me.

Helios's gaze flicks to my throat, and I can tell he can see my pulse fluttering there.

"All right, kitten." He leans down, flicking his tongue over my pulse, and my core clenches.

Helios's phone rings, and he grabs it from the coffee table. I look up at him, watching his face as he reads the messages pouring into his phone. He sits up suddenly, and I frown, pushing up on my elbows.

"Fuck. I have to go." He scrambles up, shoving his phone into his pocket. I blink up at him, sitting up.

"Go?"

Helios looks at me, emotion in his eyes at the small show of reluctance from me in that one tiny two-letter word.

"I love you," he says, bending to kiss me tenderly, more emotion in that one kiss than in any we've ever shared.

Why is he leaving?

"Fine. Bye." I cross my arms over my breasts, withdrawing from him, trying to stop the anticipatory ache in my chest at his absence.

Helios kisses me again, deeper, and then runs out the door, leaving the room dark and lonely. Like it always is when he's gone.

Chapter Twenty-Two

SELENE

I'm in trouble.

THIS COULD NOT HAVE BEEN A WORSE TIME TO GET THAT TEXT. Selene would never send such a text unless she were quite literally on the verge of death. So, of fucking course, she would send me that right as I was finally getting somewhere emotionally with Melinoë. That flicker of vulnerability in her eyes could have pushed us to a new level. But instead, I'm heading to meet my sister at our emergency bolt hole. The place we go when this world has gone tits up, and we need to hide. A place so remote, so desolate, that no one dares journey to it unless they have a desperate need.

Upstate New York.

I step inside the gothic stone mansion, frowning at the slight layer of dust over the entry table. Selene was fastidious. Even in a state of panic, she would have taken the time to clean.

"Sel?" I call out, my voice reverberating through the empty space and returning to me with the force of a blow. My unease escalates, and I close the door slowly. Solar light pools in my hand, prepared to launch with the force of a laser.

"If you've broken in," I warn, walking further into the

mansion. "You've caught me in an extremely bad mood."

The newspaper left out on the entry table draws my gaze, my brows furrowing when I see Persephone on the cover. I lean over and pick it up, scanning through the article. It's an op-ed about Persephone. Is her mother legitimately insane? I understand that Demeter now has the power of an actual Primordial, but tempting Hades to this degree? She's asking for him to make a move. We can barely keep him in the Underworld. I can't imagine how he is going to react to this.

I hear a creak from upstairs and lower the newspaper, my palms lighting up again with my power. My eyes catch on the silver hair at the top of the steps, the light in my palms dying out when I see Selene on the landing. "Selene."

I start up the stairs, but my brows furrow as I get closer to her, and I stop. She's just staring at me, waiting for me to come closer. On a hunch, I raise my hand, letting a small stream of sunlight hit her. Instead of hurting her, it breaks the illusion.

Fuck.

"If that woman couldn't convince me to your side, do you really think you will fare any better?" I snarl and whirl around, looking for the source of the illusion, but I recognize this manipulation of light. My father, Hyperion, the Titan of Light.

His disembodied voice rumbles all around me. "That woman? How disrespectful."

I spin on my heel and toss another beam of light, hitting the wall, leaving nothing but a precisely burned hole. My father doesn't suddenly appear. Small solar flares lick at my palms, and I carefully step down the stairs, letting them lick the air.

"She's no longer my mother," I hiss. I throw a few more fireballs, uncaring that I am blowing holes in the mansion. "She made her choice. She chose you."

Theia chose her husband over her kids, a husband who never loved her. They had an arranged marriage, and despite Theia's ever-faithful nature to him, Hyperion never returned her unwavering love. No matter what anyone said, she was blind to all his faults. The Titaness of Sight is unseeing when staring at the Titan of Light. The irony is not lost on me. Fate does love these mocking ironies.

"She's my wife," he mocks. "Of course, she chose me."

I shout in anger, sending out another beam through a wall, taking off the head of a framed portrait of some old white man. "Why did you lure me here if not to fight me?

Too cowardly to step out from your illusions, old man?"

His laugh makes me spin again, trying to find the source. "Who said I wanted to fight you?"

I freeze, that same unease shooting down my spine. I thought it was the initial warning of my father's presence, but no. There's something else. Why did he bring me here? I rushed here without thinking it through, just as he knew I would.

His laugh skitters down my spine before vanishing, the silence settling around me like a shroud. The hair on the nape of my neck stands on end, and I spin again, launching a concentrated beam of light at the front of the house, a smile curving my lips when part of the mansion gives way.

I stalk down the stairs, catching another flash of pale hair down the hall. I send out a powerful flare, but as the light fades, I realize the hair is not just pale but white.

Oh fuck.

Static floods the mansion, and Zeus hurls the Bolt at me, hitting me in the abdomen. Fuck. My father sold me out to the King of the Olympians. He lured me here and turned me over. The force of the Bolt throws me into the wall, the plaster collapsing around my body. Dark spots bloom across my vision as the Bolt tears through my muscles and into my organs. I forgot how much this hurts.

Zeus is on me in a blur, his fingers digging into my chest, forcing lightning through my body. I struggle, trying to break his hold on me, his fingers burning into my flesh, electricity vibrating through my bones. They broke and healed under the onslaught of the King of Gods' power.

My eyes vibrated in my sockets, unable to focus from the force of his lightning. I knew Zeus was powerful, but the last time we fought, he only had a fraction of his strength.

His grandmother, Gaia, gifted him the Bolt in the first war. The Bolt is created from lightning, the first and the last. There is no weapon more powerful in a one-on-one face-off. With most of my solar power severed, I am no match against him.

Run. I needed to run. Somehow. Melinoë. I can't die. I haven't heard her lie about loving me yet. Roaring, I unleash what is left of my solar power, blinding Zeus. It's enough to force him to release me and send him panting and stumbling blindly away from the piercing light. I flash to the first place I can focus on.

I slam against her front door and groan. Right, adamantium, and I can't flash through it in my state. I knock hard on it, the blood coating my fingers and dripping gold rivulets down her front door.

"Melinoë!" I shout, my voice wavering. She's here, she has to be here. I lean heavily against the door, holding a hand to my abdomen, trying to keep my intestines inside my stomach cavity as I heal. If they fall out before my healing kicks in completely, it will be days before I recover. Bolts from the King of the Gods are a fucking bitch to heal from. My legs tremble, and I fall to my knees, pressing my head to her door. I smack my palm against the metal.

I should have stayed with Melinoë. Why did I ever leave her side?

My vision flickers. Should have stayed…

Chapter Twenty-Three
Melinoë

I GLIDE MY FINGERS ALONG THE SURFACE OF THE MILKY BATHWATER. The bubbles are long gone, and so is the warmth. The room is silent save for the small plunking noise the drops make when they fall from the tap. In my head, Helios repeats those treacherous three words, the eight letters of doom. He left hours ago, yet the apartment still feels thick with it.

I hear a knock at the door, and I know it's him, though something sounds off. There is the absence of his usual arrogance. The undertone of "I'm here, pay attention to me". But I still don't move, not ready to leave the serenity of my bath. I lift my hand, tilting my head as I watch the water droplets fall from my fingers, rippling the otherwise still water before merging with the larger body.

As my eyes wander, trailing along the cream porcelain of the tub, my mind drifts back. I usually don't let myself dwell, but in this moment, my past seems safer than my future. I take a deep breath, hold the air in my lungs, and slide down the back of the tub, fully submerging myself.

My stockpile of wood is gone, and I already feel the dread curling around my stomach. I need to make a journey into the woods again. I usually try to do this only when the moon is in its

darkest phase, but as I look up, it mocks me by pressing its white shining light down on me. The dark indentations look more like a sinister smile the longer I gaze upon it. I force my eyes away before they start to talk to me. They always talk if I stare too long.

Mud coats my skin, leaving almost none of it showing, and I consider the next time I will be able to make my way to the river Styx for a wash. The brown water never leaves me very clean, but it helps with the itching. The beings within taunt me as I rub at my face, but they never pull me in. They've never even tried. Maybe I'm too mad even for the abyss.

I prepare myself to leave, planning on gathering as much as I can, even though this will be a risky forage. I braid my hair, noting that the left side has a few more white strands than it did the previous night. No doubt they are thanks to the nightmares that plagued me as I descended into the darkness, enticed by the promises the voices made to me. It was another trick, of course. This time, when I became aware again, I was surrounded by eighteen tarantulas the size of a house, and my leg still throbbed from where one of them had bitten me.

A twig snaps from the mouth of my cave, and my head snaps up. I let the darkness seep out of me, dousing the cave into the blackness of my mind.

"Mellie..." a weak voice called, followed by a flicker of light.

This is wrong. This isn't how the memory goes...

I lurch up in the bath, my lungs burning as I gulp the air, bathwater sluicing down my sides. My pulse thunders in my ears, but I strain, listening for Helios's knock. I wait a moment, then another, but there is nothing. Unease sits heavy on my shoulders, the same feeling I grew so used to in my past life. I slip from the bathtub, wrap a black towel around myself, and leave the bathroom, frowning at the front door. Something's wrong.

My gaze narrows on the deep purple of the wood, and my heart lurches when I notice the gilded pool seeping into the carpet at the bottom of the door. I yank it open, and my whole body tenses when I see Helios slumped on the floor, a large trench of a wound across his abdomen.

"Helios? Fuck." I drop to my knees, cupping his cheeks, inspecting him for more wounds before I focus on the main one.

"Hey… kitten." Helios smiles weakly, his eyes glazed but fixed on my face.

I curse again, pressing down on his abdomen, trying to staunch the bleeding. "What the fuck happened?"

He winces. "My sisters. They texted me… needing help."

"Shit, shit, shit." I stand and slide my arms under his, yanking him back into the apartment. I groan at the effort, wishing I was stronger. Helios's eyes become heavier. Every one of his blinks seems to last longer.

"Keep talking," I snarl, pulling his deadweight across the wood floors, leaving a trail of golden ichor.

I prop him up against the couch, grabbing his t-shirt from our earlier tryst and pressing it against his open wound.

"You're pretty," Helios drawls, his lips pulled into a weak smirk.

I'd love to see his arrogant smirk right now.

His head sags slightly to the side, and I grab his face, forcing him to focus on me. "Who did this to you?"

His eyes flicker slightly. "Zeus."

"Oh, is that so?" I feel my lips pull into a wicked smile. I've been waiting for an excuse to beat the shit out of that piece of shit. I'm sure Persephone would love to join me in cutting off his balls and sending them to Hera.

Helios groans, and I look back at the wound. It's healing slowly, too slowly. He probably needs stitches.

"Helios?" I look up at him, noticing that he's already passed out. Probably from the pain or blood loss. Who knows?

His face is so peaceful in sleep, all the arrogance and ego gone. In sleep, he truly looks like the most perfect of summer days. I brush a lock of hair from his forehead but yank my hand away when I leave a trail of his blood in the wake of my fingers.

My touch changes the vision of the daydream. The nightmare encroaches upon it, bending it, ruining it. Nightmares and daydreams are opposites. They are never to be crossed. So why am I sitting here, looking at my own dream? I know I need to leave. My darkness will do nothing but destroy him. But I can't walk away.

I place my hands on his arms and shadow us into the bed before hurrying through to the bathroom and grabbing my small first aid kit. When I first came up here, I taught myself how to suture for the times I descended and woke up with deep gashes on my arms or legs from the nightmares.

Helios hasn't moved on the bed, and I silently hope that he stays asleep for this. I'm not sure how many stitches it will take to close him up, but I know it'll be a fair few. I clean the wound and swallow hard. It's not Helios. It's not Helios.

His body is cool, and it is so wrong. I am not used to him feeling anything but perfectly warm. As the suture tugs through the muscle, I'm vaguely aware of the voices whispering to me. Some of them are bolder now, knowing Helios is indisposed and unable to ward them off with his light.

"Don't worry, sunboy. I'll make Zeus regret this," I whisper to him as I tie the final stitch, tugging it to ensure it'll hold.

I wash my hands and take off his bloody clothes before wrapping a thick bandage around his waist. I lie down beside him, occasionally dabbing his forehead with a cool flannel. His body keeps heating to a dangerous degree as he burns through any infection and starts to heal.

Helios sleeps for hours, mumbling and twitching in his fevered state. In that time, I change his bandage twice, clean the blood from the floor in the living room and hall, and make him one of his favorite smoothies. I manage to stay awake until around three am, but exhaustion tugs at me, and I fall into sleep, surrounded by his scent.

"Kitten?" His voice fills my unconsciousness, and I tighten my arms around the sunshine-scented hard pillow I'm curled against. I dive into my powers, needing to protect the muscular body next to me. Strong hands cup my cheek, followed by his honeyed voice. "Kitten?"

I lift my chin, unwilling to leave the bliss of warm slumber holding me captive. Soft, perfectly warm lips press against mine, and I moan, tightening my hold. The body in my arms tenses, and my eyes fly open. Helios's caramel eyes lock on mine, and awareness rushes into me. The blood. The wound. The stitches.

I spring up, looking him over. "What's wrong? Are you okay?"

Helios shifts and winces. "Did you stitch me up, hellcat?"

I brush his hand away, unraveling the bandages to check his stitches. The bleeding has slowed down, and the stitches are holding well.

Helios cups my cheek. "Hey." I ignore him, cleansing the

wound again. Helios brushes my hair back. "How long was I out?" Helios asks, and I can feel his gaze on me.

I glance at the clock on the bedside table, careful not to look at him. Not ready to see whatever it is I know I'm going to see in his eyes, but mostly not ready for him to see it reflected in mine.

"Nine hours."

"Fuck." Helios takes a deep breath. "I don't remember getting here. Did I say anything?"

"Just your usual weird, mushy shit," I reply, my lips twitching slightly.

Helios's laughs morphs into a groan of pain. "Fuck, those bolts sting."

My gaze flashes to his, and I can feel the fury in my eyes reflect off him. "I'm the only one who gets to stab you. Got it?" I snarl.

Helios smiles softly. "Got it. Although he didn't stab me."

"Well. No one except me can maim you, either," I growl.

Helios nods, his eyes sparkling. "I promise it won't happen again."

I look away, concentrating on wrapping his wound again. "I made you one of those weird, gross smoothies you like to stick your cock in or whatever."

Helios chuckles, more carefully this time, to avoid tugging at the stitches. "So much care. Who are you, and what have you done with my girlfriend?"

I growl, poking him in the chest. "I am not, have never been, and will never be. Your fucking girlfriend." I shadow the smoothie into my hand and thrust it at him. "Drink this before I shove it down your urethra."

His answering pout makes my lips tilt, and he takes a long sip of his gross salad drink. My chest warms at the sight of him awake and that look in his eyes. I stand up and turn away from him.

"Come back." I can practically hear him reaching out for me.

"Drink your smoothie," I reply, disappearing into the bathroom. I press my back against the door and lean my head against it, closing my eyes.

"Baby?"

A tear slides down my cheek, and I frown at the sensation, collecting the moisture on my finger. I watch as it slides from one finger to the other, and then I lick the small drop, my brows furrowing more at the salty taste of it.

"Mellie?" Helios's voice sounds concerned and pained. The moron has probably sat up and pulled at his stitches. I wipe any residue of tears from my face before leaving the bathroom to glare at Helios. "Stop moving. You're slowing the healing."

"You were gone." Helios pouts, reaching for me.

Needy fucker. I walk back over to him, his fingers trailing down my thigh as soon as I'm in arm's reach.

"I'm going to contact Apollo," I say, frowning down at his wound.

"No," Helios growls. "Can't be in the same room as him."

"Why?"

"We overlap too much. Solar flare."

I roll my eyes at the macho dramatic bullshit.

"Okay, well, maybe I could go meet him. Get you something for healing."

Helios shakes his head. "Stay with me." He slides his hand into mine, and I look at how his fingers perfectly entwine with mine.

"Helios…"

"Stay."

He tugs me closer, cupping my cheek. "I'm a Titan, Melinoë. I'll be fine."

I frown at him, but he pulls me closer and brushes his lips over mine. "You bandaged me."

As usual, I can't stop myself from kissing him back, but I pull back after a few long moments.

"Yes, well, you were bleeding all over everything," I growl, glaring at him. "It was annoying."

Helios's smile fills the whole room, brighter than the sun. "So annoying."

"Ugh. Don't start glowing again," I groan, rolling my eyes.

He glows brighter. "Me? Never."

I shove his shoulder, taking care not to hurt him. "Stop. I should have let you bleed out."

Helios's grin widens. "You couldn't. You care for me."

"Gross. Do not." I glare, crossing my arms across my chest.

Helios pointedly looks at his wound, then at me, lifting an eyebrow. "You absolutely do."

Arrogant asshole.

Chapter Twenty-Four

Helios

S HE STITCHED ME UP. TENDED MY WOUNDS, and fuck, that shouldn't mean so much to me, but this is Melinoë. She was just as likely to stab me as to stitch me, and here she is hovering over me like a concerned nurse. A sexy, sexy nurse who lets the patients run the hospital… I even regained consciousness with her pressed into me. What more could I possibly want in life? Even her eyes were more vulnerable, less guarded with me. She's alert to my every breath and wince. I'm tempted to rip out my stitches again, so she has to stay and give me more care.

Melinoë grabs her phone, ordering a chicken salad for me, along with pizza and thirty Diablo-flavored chicken wings for herself. She glares at me even as she settles in and turns the television on. It is the only thing in her entire apartment that is not partially destroyed. Even the sheets I am lying on are torn, the mattress lumpy and uneven in places. Her clothes are strewn in every direction, various knives sticking out from some of the piles. I should clean the place up a little when she dozes off. The home renovation show begins, and I wince as I shift to cuddle into her.

"I don't think so," she hisses at me. I am not sure if she's mad at me for wincing or cuddling her, but it is probably the latter.

"But I'm injured," I say, sticking my lower lip out for effect.

"And if you try that cuddling shit with me again, you'll get more injured," she warns, glaring at me.

So it was the cuddling, then. I knew it. Turning slightly away from her, I let out an exaggerated groan and cradle my abdomen. She curses. "Fine. You can have thirty seconds."

I smirk and cuddle into her side. She grumbles and reluctantly wraps an arm around me. I press into her side, resting my head on her chest. After a few moments of silence, I whisper, "It was a trap."

She tenses but doesn't say anything, still holding me against her side.

"I thought my sisters were in trouble," I continue, thinking back. "My father can manipulate light, and all sight is based on it. His illusions make you doubt everything. They're so seamless." Melinoë doesn't move. She barely breathes, just listening. I can't remember the last time someone just listened to me. "He lured me there, and then he set me up. The second before Zeus smited me, he bailed."

I don't know why I didn't see it coming before. Maybe my mother's plea had thrown me off so much that even when I knew it was my father, I didn't immediately flash away. Instead, I stayed to fight with him like a fucking idiot. Normally, I wouldn't have bothered. Why try to change things that I can't? I can't make my father care more or my mother care less. But something about him using Selene's distress got under my skin. I was already trying to pick between the two warring sides, but this was a solid mark against the Titan faction. Although my current injury is from the King of the Olympians, so that is another mark against the Olympians.

How do I choose? If it were just my life, I would throw in with Melinoë without a second thought, but it's not just me. I have to be careful when my sister's lives also hang in the balance. Melinoë gently grasps my jaw, drawing my focus, tilting my face to hers.

"They're going to start rounding up Titans," I admit. If they haven't already.

Her eyes flicker before she leans in and licks my cheek. The move is so her that it makes me relax. How could I be thinking about the future when I'm lying in bed with my insanely hot girlfriend, who just took the time to stitch up my wounds?

"Thank you, baby." I give her a small smile and reach up to cup her cheek, stroking it with my thumb. "I'm sorry I scared you."

"Nothing scares me, asshole," she snaps back, but her eyes show her relief. I must have really terrified her, showing up with a gaping wound and intestines about to slip out.

I keep my eyes on her. "I love you."

Her eyes flicker again, and I glimpse the emotions lurking there before she masks them. "Fuck you and that phrase."

She's not outright denying it anymore or telling me to shut up. Progress. I kiss the side of her neck.

She groans but doesn't move away. "You're obsessed with me. It's really weird."

She still doesn't move away. If anything, she leans into me a bit more. I shift to change our positions so she's cuddled into my side, her hand resting gently on my chest, above my wounds. Her fingers unerringly find the fingerprints left behind by Zeus's power, stroking them as they continue to fade. "I know you're really into me, too. It's embarrassing."

She sneers. "Ew. No, I am not. I barely tolerate you."

I kiss her head. "Such a liar."

Before she can respond, her phone alerts, and she pulls away. Right, the food. My stomach grumbles, reminding me exactly how starved I am.

Chapter Twenty-Five
Melinoë

I HAND HELIOS HIS BOX OF LEAVES, GRIMAC-ING AT THE THOUGHT OF EATING SOME-THING SO...GREEN. I hand Helios his box of leaves, grimacing at the thought of eating something so…green. But he smiles widely at me, taking the box and tugging me closer to him to kiss me.

I just roll my eyes in response, climbing on the bed and opening the pizza box. The sight is truly beautiful. Greasy and cheesy. I marvel at the cheese pull as I grab a slice and take a large bite, moaning softly. Why do I never realize how hungry I am until I'm eating?

"Thanks for the meal, baby," Helios croons into my ear as he strokes my hair.

I bristle at the pet name, but his fingers running through my hair calms me like I'm some damn house cat. I hold the slice of pizza to his lips, and he surprises me by taking a large bite.

"Delicious." He grins around his bite.

"Better than green, leafy garbage." I snort, turning my attention to the television.

Helios and I eat in comfortable silence, watching the show, both of us captivated by the home renovations unfolding in front of us. I grab the box of hot wings and tuck in, uncaring that my fingers are getting covered in the sticky, dark sauce. I drop the last bone back in the box, and Helios grabs my wrist, bringing my hand to his mouth and sucking on my fingers. My lips part slightly as his tongue curls around the pads. Helios takes his time, sucking on each of my fingers before releasing them from his mouth, his lips tipped up in a smile. I look away, pulling my hand free. Why does he so easily make me weak in the knees?

The news flashes up on screen, and Helios glances at the TV.

"Shit, it's Wednesday?"

I nod, blinking at him. "Why?"

"I heard through the grapevine that there's going to be an op-ed about Persephone in Olympus Today!. I believe it drops today."

"How do I get it?" I ask, kneeling beside him.

"I have a subscription. It'll be delivered to my apartment today." Helios tries to get up and groans in pain. Gold splotches bloom on his bandage, and I hiss, pushing him back down.

"Don't move. I'll go. You keep eating and healing." I glare at him. "If you move, so help me gods, I will turn your appendix into an earring and pierce it into your eyeball," I growl, and my gaze travels back to his wound. It's healing too slowly.

"Stop flirti—"

I don't even wait to hear the end of his sentence before shadowing to his apartment. The large open space is light, the sun streaming through the windows. I quickly leaf through his mail, chucking everything that doesn't resemble a newspaper to the side. When I realize it's not there, I curse and walk to his kitchen island.

My gaze snags on something that could resemble a newspaper, and I snatch it up. I begin to unroll it, but I'm distracted by a piece of paper fluttering to the floor. I frown and pick it up. The script is feminine and pretty.

Call me.

-S

S? I narrow my eyes at the note, crumpling it in my clenched fists. I will deal with that later. In order to kill him, I need him to be healed. To make it fair. I shove the newspaper and the now very crumpled note into my pocket and shadow to Apollo's house.

I've only been here once before, with Hades years ago. He'd asked me to accompany him to discuss some business with the God of Healing and to say I was unimpressed would be an understatement. He is one of a few divines who decided to branch out and achieve celebrity status. Honestly, his head and ego almost match Helios's, though I think he may be more insufferable.

The last time I was here, he pretended I didn't exist, which was perfect, especially since I felt the undeniable urge to prank the god mercilessly. I believe there had been some complaints to Hades about his "weird gothic plus one" having stolen a few precious artifacts and ruining some of his coveted clothes.

I didn't ruin them. I just wrote some fun messages that would only be seen in the flash of a camera.

Messages like "I have a small cock" and "Ask me about my butt plug". It was harmless fun, but I will be good today, and Apollo will give me what I want if he knows what's good for him.

I knock on the door sweetly, just like a girl scout trying to sell cookies. Apollo doesn't answer right away, and I roll my eyes, knowing everything with him is about power.

I hold back another eye roll and a snort of disgust when he finally does grace me with his presence. He is shirtless, wearing checkered boxers and a dark maroon robe that he's left open.

"Well, well, if it isn't Hades' little Wednesday Addams," Apollo says by way of greeting, his eyebrow raised. "Here to destroy more of my things?"

I grin, pushing the door open and marching past him into the most ridiculous room I've ever seen. "If you're offering…" I say, grabbing an expensive-looking stone statue from a shelf just inside the room and tossing it in the air, catching it easily.

Apollo growls, snatching it from my hand. "What have I done to deserve the pleasure of your company?" His lips are pulled into a tight smile, his teeth clenched.

Fuck, I love getting under people's skin. The madness inside me croons. Apollo might not be afraid of much, but I make him uneasy, and it's fucking delectable.

I smile sweetly at him, tilting my head. "I need a healing ointment."

Apollo's expression of annoyance quickly melts into one of intrigue, and he lifts a brow. "Oh? Is that so?"

I nod once, not enjoying that I have to ask for help from someone, so… Apollo.

Apollo quickly looks me over, lifting his chin. "You are

not injured."

I roll my eyes. "No shit."

"So why the ointment?" He studies me in a way that makes me want to rip my face off.

"Because I need it," I snap at him, clenching my fists.

Apollo's lips tug into a smile. "For someone else. Does the Goddess of Nightmares… care for someone?"

I cross my arms. "Maybe it's for Hades. Or Persephone."

"But it's not. Hades would have reached out to me if it were for himself, a simple text. And if it were for his queen, he would have been blowing up my phone." Apollo circles me. "Besides, everyone knows Persephone is currently on Olympus. With her mother."

"Against her will," I snarl.

"That may be so, but there are powerful healers on Olympus. In fact, Demeter has healers in her employ. Her mother wouldn't let little old me anywhere near Persephone," Apollo drones on.

He definitely likes the sound of his own voice.

"No. This is for someone else," Apollo continues. "Someone you care about. Isn't that right, Melinoë? Maybe someone you… love?"

I whirl on him, snarling, "Take that back."

Apollo laughs, fueling my anger. "Well, this is an interesting development. Something to file away."

"Are you threatening me?"

"Threatening? Absolutely not. I think it's cute that you have fallen for someone. I just hope they know what they're in for."

I narrow my eyes at him. "Are you going to give me the ointment or not?"

Apollo quirks a brow. "Tell me who it's for, and I'll give it to you."

Fuck. How close is Apollo to his dad? Can I risk giving Zeus Helios's location?

"I'm waiting, black parade."

I glare at him. "This information goes no further, or you won't have to worry about Hades' wrath. You will feel mine." I'm not sure what Apollo sees in my eyes at that moment, but he pales, and I can feel the fear flickering within him.

He nods once, watching me carefully.

"Helios. The ointment is for Helios."

Apollo blinks. "Well fuck. I wasn't expecting that."

"The ointment, Apollo," I grate out, my patience razor

thin.

He disappears to collect ingredients, and I wander into his bathroom to wash my face. Being around the divine has never been my favorite. It sets me even more on edge than usual. I scrub my face and use the most expensive-looking towel to dry my skin. I look at myself in the mirror, focusing on my eyes. They're still clear, but I can see the effect being here is having on me.

I open his medicine cabinets and rifle through the contents, my brows raising when I find a pink razor and… hair removal cream. My lips pull into a wicked smile, and I grab it from the shelf before locating his shampoo. When I open the bottle, I'm hit with the overpowering scent of green apple and pear. I dump some of the liquid down the sink, and it falls from the bottle like liquid gold, proving how expensive it is. Once I have removed around half, I open the bottle of hair removal cream and pour it in, shaking the shampoo bottle to combine.

"Say goodbye to those pretty long blond locks, dick."

"Melinoë?" I hear Apollo call, his voice uncertain.

I return everything to its rightful place and leave the bathroom, finding the living room empty once again. Apollo appears less than a moment later, coming from a different corridor. He eyes me suspiciously, and I hold my hands up innocently.

"I wasn't anywhere near your clothes."

He glares and chucks a small gold pot at me. "Here. Apply liberally and tell him to take it easy for the next few hours."

I catch it easily, nodding. "Thanks! See ya hopefully never." I leave his apartment, the hair on my skin standing on end at the feeling of his fear and apprehension.

I shadow back into my apartment, finding Helios lying exactly where I left him. His golden eyes find mine, and my heart thrums a little. I pull the paper and the note out of my pocket.

"You found it?" Helios smiles widely, looking at me like his world begins and ends with me.

I force my face into a glare, throwing the crumpled piece of paper at him. "S is just desperate for you to call her." I discard the paper to the side and start roughly tugging at his bandages. "Also, I got healing ointment."

Helios shifts so he can look at the note.

"Don't move," I growl.

"Baby," Helios says, "S is for Selene. My sister."

"Dont care." But I feel most of the tension lifting from

my shoulders. I open the pot, my nose wrinkling at the smell. The goo is milky white and smells earthy and sharp. I smear it on his wound, and it tingles against my fingertips.

Helios watches me, but his gaze wanders to the newspaper. I hiss when he snatches for it, his wound seeping blood when he does.

"Shit!" Helios hisses.

"What?" I look at the cover and see a photo of Persephone that spans nearly the entire front page. She looks nothing like my best friend. Given what Helios had reported about her, I expected it, yet seeing her with my own eyes breaks something in me. I snatch it from him and read the title, but my head spins, the words blending. I blink, trying to focus and gasp when I finally comprehend the headline.

HIDDEN ROSE, GODDESS OF SPRING SEEKS ELIGIBLE BACHELOR.

Helios looks at the paper with similar horror, and I flip to the article.

PERSEPHONE PROSPERINA, THE ROSE OF OLYMPUS, HAS MADE HER DEBUT INTO SOCIETY, AND IT HAS ROCKED THE WHOLE REALM. THE GREAT AND MIGHTY DEMETER VERY KINDLY ALLOWED US TO INTERVIEW HER DELIGHTFUL DAUGHTER AND WAS EVEN SO KIND AS TO ALLOW US AN EXCLUSIVE. WHEN ASKED WHY SHE KEPT SUCH A LOVELY SECRET FOR ALL THESE YEARS, DEMETER STATED, "THE WORLD WAS NOT DESERVING OF MY PRIZED PERSEPHONE. BUT NOW IT IS TIME FOR HER TO MAKE HER DEBUT INTO SOCIETY. IT WAS ALWAYS MY PLAN TO INTRODUCE HER, BUT THIS WAS DELAYED DUE TO UNFORESEEN EVENTS." WHILE HER GREATNESS WAS UNABLE TO DELVE DEEPER INTO HER REASONING, THE JOY THAT MISS PROSPERINA BRINGS INSPIRES HAPPINESS NOW THAT SHE IS BEING SHARED WITH US. BEFORE CONTINUING TO THE DELIGHTFUL INTERVIEW, IT BRINGS ALL OF US AT OLYMPUS TODAY! GREAT PRIDE TO MAKE ANOTHER EXCLUSIVE ANNOUNCEMENT. HER GREATNESS DEMETER IS NOW ALLOWING SUITORS TO COME FORWARD FOR THE HAND OF HER MOST BELOVED DAUGHTER. SHOULD ANY OF THE GENTLEMEN OF OLYMPUS WANT TO PURSUE THE BEAUTY, THEY SHOULD MAKE THEIR INTEREST KNOWN TO DEMETER.

I snarl, throwing the paper. "Fuck! How am I meant to show that to Hades?" I stand from the bed, pacing, my blood surging in fury.

"He's already losing his shit," Helios adds unhelpfully.

I scoop up the front page of the paper, brushing my fingers over the photo of the ghost of my best friend. "He'll want to dream walk again." And I need to help him, regardless of the dangers to myself or them. They're already going through hell.

Helios nods and sits up with a groan. My eyes snap to him. "You need to bring me with you."

"You need to sleep off this injury. I don't care if I need to knock you out." I gently push him back on the bed.

"Well, unless you're planning to knock me unconscious, I don't sleep."

I give him a look. "You were sleeping before."

Helios laughs. "I was half dead." I bristle, and Helios smiles at me. "Just cuddle me." He opens his arms, and I growl at him but reluctantly move into his arms.

"You want to know the positive in being unable to sleep?" Helios asks, kissing my head.

"What?"

Helios strokes my hair. "No nightmares."

I tense, the truth slipping out as the softest of whispers. "I'm the nightmare."

Helios cups my cheek, tilting my head up. "You're a dream to me."

I search his eyes. The room is thick with feeling, so dense it's choking me. I swallow, trying to push down the feeling of my heart racing in my chest.

"St-stop being obsessed with me," I stammer, trying to harden my gaze.

"Melinoë. You don't have to do that with me." Helios strokes my cheek.

"Do what?"

"Pretend to be hard. You can be soft with me. I promise I won't tell anyone."

Gods, he has to stop looking at me like that. I growl softly. "I'm not soft."

"Only sometimes," Helios says, his lips pulling into a half-smile.

"You're the ooey-gooey one. Not me."

"I'm like the perfect brownie."

"And I'm like a cactus," I growl again, glaring at him. "A poisonous one."

Helios's laugh is like honey. "No. You're like bone marrow." I blink, but Helios continues, "You're tough on the outside, but when cooked just right, your inside is ooey-gooey."

"Well, you'll never cook me well enough to find out." I

pout, crossing my arms.

"That right?" Helios smirks.

He's such an arrogant asshole. I grab his face, kissing him deeply, and Helios immediately responds, cupping my head.

"Baby?" Helios groans into my mouth. I pull his bottom lip between my teeth. "Fuck. I wish I was healed enough to fuck you."

I press my body against his side, grinding against his thigh just enough that there's a little pressure against my clit.

"Maybe you can just ride me, and we just ignore when my stitches inevitably break." Helios moans, digging his fingers into my ass. He tilts slightly, trying to get closer, but groans in pain when he snaps a stitch. I curse, pulling back.

Helios searches for my lips with his. "Ignore it."

I pull back. "You're bleeding, and I did not cause it."

"But I'm horny, and you caused that. So… priorities." Helios moans, still trying to kiss me.

I kiss him again but pull back after a minute. "Helios…"

"You better fuck me, or I'll think you love me or something." Helios digs his fingers more into me, his eyes sparkling with need.

I lean in, hovering my lips over his. "Helios? Until you can pin me to the mattress and fuck me without bleeding all over me from a wound I didn't cause, we're not fucking," I say, grabbing the pot with the ointment and slathering more on his wound.

"But…" Helios pouts.

"No sex," I growl, wrapping a new bandage around his waist.

"But I like sex," Helios whines like a petulant child being told they can't have more ice cream.

"Yes, well. You also like being healed."

"But it's worth it for me—"

"No." I yank the bandage tighter, making him wince, and my lips twitch.

Helios shifts slightly. "You want to hear something super ooey-gooey?"

"No. Never." I finish tying the bandage.

"I like being injured because I like you tending to me." Helios smirks, watching my hands brush over his abs.

"You won't like it when you hear the payment." I glare at him.

"I can pay in kisses?" Helios puckers his lips, and I roll

my eyes.

"Seven Helios-free days," I reply, ignoring his beckoning full lips.

"Nope," Helios says, crossing his arms, but then he softens. "Baby?"

I look at him, slightly guarded.

"We're going to get her back."

Where did that come from? Though I'm glad for the reassurance, I look away. I can't get the image of her out of my mind, trapped, both physically and mentally.

"Mel. Tell me what you're thinking." Helios forces me to look at him, and I bristle slightly.

"How much I hate you. Stop calling me baby. I prefer evil demon spawn."

"My baby evil demon spawn girlfriend," Helios says, kissing me softly.

I glare at him, looking at the photo of Persephone again. "Fuck. How am I going to break the news to demon daddy?"

"I don't know. But we need to do it and soon. It looks like Demeter is expecting this to be a quick turnaround."

I nod once. "I'll tell him tomorrow." I look at Helios. "You need to rest. That's what Apollo said."

"Rest with me?"

I roll my eyes but curl into his side.

"So you went to Apollo then?" Helios asks into my hair. I nod. "He's a dick."

"Yeah? Did he ruffle my baby's feathers?" I hear the amusement in Helios's voice. He's a dick too.

I look up at him, giving him a scathing look. "He's an arrogant prick, but it's fine. I had my fun."

Helios lifts an eyebrow, running his fingers through my hair.

"I added hair removal cream into his shampoo."

Helios bursts out laughing and pulls my face to his, kissing me hard. "Fuck, you're so fucking amazing."

I deepen the kiss, moaning into him, but pull back after a moment, remembering his wound. Helios pouts for a few moments but grabs the remote for the TV and turns on Extreme Hoarders. It's not long before I relax into him, falling asleep.

WITH EVERY PASSING MOMENT, MY SIDE HEALS A BIT MORE. I wince as I pull a stitch out, letting my skin knit closed. Melinoë is pretty handy with a needle and thread, which seems odd given the torn state of most of her clothes. Maybe she can only sew when it comes to skin. For some reason, that thought makes my lips twitch. It sounds exactly like Melinoë.

She stretches in sleep next to me, nuzzling into my side. "Love you."

The sleepy words make my skin glow, and this time, it's completely involuntary. My emotions simply taking control. "Yes, you do," I purr softly.

Maybe one day I'll actually hear her say the words while she's conscious, but I don't truly need them from her. There's something so clear about her feelings for me in her actions. Maybe it's the way she naturally acts toward others that makes it apparent how different she is with me. The words are in her every action, every look. I hear them every time her face softens a bit when she thinks I'm not watching, then hardens just as fast when she catches herself. Each time, my heart thuds against my ribcage. So, no, I don't really need to hear the words from her. There are things in this world that exist with complete certainty.

I kiss her head before pulling out my phone and texting

Eos.

Our beloved sperm donor attempted to trap me by pretending to be Sel.

Selene's number must have been spoofed or replicated, so I can't text her without the message potentially being lost along the way.

I was about to text you.

Unease turns my stomach. Eos is more compassionate than that. She would ask for all the details of such an incident. So for her to completely ignore what I said…

What's happened?

Melinoë digs her fingers into me again, and I have a flashback to another time when she'd lain curled against me plays through my head. I texted my sisters then, too. Is this another time when history will repeat itself? A time when we think we have free will only to play out the destiny written for us long before we were born?

They caught Mom.

My body tightens instinctively, and then I remember

who exactly I am fretting for.

H

Don't care.

There might be a part of my heart that longs to protect my mother, but the greater part of me remembers all the time she chose to protect a man who cared nothing for her over her own children. But Eos is the softest of us, the most forgiving. I burn bright, and Selene can freeze hearts, but Eos is in between us. She is warm and inviting, while Selene and I are the extremes.

E

Olympus is abuzz with the news,
the Titaness of Sight captured.
It's noteworthy.

I look at Melinoë, stroking her hair back from her face. What do I care? I have a very small list of people I truly care about. In fact, I can count them on a single hand, and the Titaness of Sight is decidedly not on that list.

Melinoë sinks her teeth into my chest in sleep, tearing the skin. I muffle the moan that immediately follows. The wound on my abs is close to being healed, and at the moment, I do not give a fuck if it tears open and I bleed to death. Right now, with Melinoë curled into me, I don't have any responsibilities, no choices to be made.

"Baby," I groan when she licks her bite mark on my chest.

Her eyes flutter open, both completely black. I knew she was awake. I roll to pin her beneath me, looming over her.

"Your wound," she whispers, even as she wraps her legs around my waist, keeping me locked to her.

I press my lips to hers, biting the lower one until it splits, filling my mouth with her golden ichor. "Fuck, my wound."

It is almost healed anyway. She digs her nails into my back, splitting my flesh. I moan at the pain, arching into the exquisite sensation of my blood pooling on my back. She coats her palm and fingers with the golden ichor and brings it to my throat. I lift my chin, stretching my neck so she can press her bloody hand against me, marking me in one more way.

Thank fuck I'm already naked. I push up the big torn shirt Melinoë is wearing and groan when I see she's not wearing any panties. I lock my eyes on her and press my cock to her entrance, feeling her wetness coat my sensitive tip. My tongue forms filthy words as I thrust hard into her dripping cunt, but none of them make it past my lips.

Even though I love talking dirty to her, and I love it even more when she talks back to me, I want the only sounds to be our bodies colliding and our heavy breaths. Sometimes, especially with Melinoë, the eye contact is more intimate than her taking my cock inside of her. It takes sex to a new level of emotional intensity between us. It is compounded by her hand covered in my blood and squeezing my throat as I fuck her.

She raises her knees along my sides, allowing me to hit deeper and grind my hips so she bruises from the force, but I refuse to close my eyes, never breaking eye contact with her. I can see the remnants of the madness lingering in the depths of her gaze, but each moment, she feels more grounded and back in her mind. It's almost a tangible shift as she roots herself in the moment with me. I keep telling her not to go where I can't follow, but the truth is, every time she loses herself to her mind, I'll bring her back, and if I can't bring her back… I'll find a way to join her in the darkness.

Even as we come, our connection never dims, never breaks. I'm not sure either of us even blinks. I shudder as she slowly lowers her hand from my throat, leaving behind a warm imprint of where her fingers.

"I love you," I pant.

She hisses. "Had to ruin it."

Melinoë shoves me off her and gets up to get ready to head to the Underworld. She pulls on a large sweater, ripped tights, and combat boots. I prop myself up on my elbows to watch her.

"Do you know what you're going to say to Hades?" I ask, watching the chaotic way she dresses herself.

She taps her lip in thought. "Sorry, demon daddy, your wife is being sold to the highest bidder and is probably about to become a bigamist." She pulls off the large sweater and picks up a dress with holes in it instead.

"If you're going to dreamwalk, I should be there." She doesn't respond, her focus on the mirror as she carefully applies her black lipstick and puts her hair into two buns. "Baby?" I prompt softly, waiting for her eyes to connect with mine in the mirror's reflection. "Don't go where I can't follow."

There's a moment of tenderness before she masks it with hostility. "I-I'm sure your weirdo stalker ass would find me even if I went into the heart of Tartarus."

Easily.

Instead of giving me a chance to respond, she shadows away from her seat, the lipstick rolling on the vanity with her hasty exit. She knew what I was going to say. Like I said, some things in this world are certain.

Chapter Twenty-Seven
Melinoë

THE DREAMWALK AFTER I SHOWED HADES THE NEWSPAPER WENT BETTER than I expected, given his heightened emotions, and tonight was even more seamless. As expected, Persephone's dreams are like an open door, both entering and exiting. It is as if she is leaving them open for Hades to waltz into.

That's my girl. This is her way of rebelling. This is that little voice in her head telling her something is wrong. I still felt the toll of it, but it was much less taxing. I pace in my apartment, wondering why, if it was easier, then why the fuck did I kiss Helios and press my forehead to his like some love-sick puppy? The memory of it makes my stomach twist, yet at the time, it felt like the most natural thing in the world.

I sit heavily on my couch, cupping my head in both hands and rocking slightly. Helios knocks at the door, just as I expected he would, but I feel my stomach twist and knot tightly. Fuck. He's going to read into this and think I like him.

Helios knocks again. "Baby?" he calls softly. I stand and walk to the door, yanking it open.

"I didn't mean to do the head thing, okay? It just happened." My words come out in an anxious rush.

Helios's lips tug into a smile, and he steps closer, pressing his forehead to mine for a moment. "Even?"

His caramel gaze locks on mine, and I blink up at him. I close my eyes but don't pull away as I planned. I feel myself relaxing, my whole body exhaling in relief. "Yes."

Helios runs his hands down my arms but pulls back after a moment. I open my eyes and peek up at him. "Want to go on a date?" he asks.

I shrug. "Sure, with who?"

Helios smirks. "With me."

"Gross, no." I roll my eyes. "I'd rather eat my own eyeballs."

Helios laughs. "Not even if it involved shooting a bunch of mortals with paintballs?"

I grin, my interest piqued. I consider for a moment and then lift my chin. "Fine. We can go on a date if you agree to three things."

"What would they be?" Helios smirks.

"First, this does not make me your girlfriend," I say, holding up one finger. "Second, you take me to dinner after, and you have to order the greasiest, most unhealthy thing on the menu." I hold up a second finger. "And third, you finally accept that I hate you and wish you'd self-implode into a black hole already," I finish, holding up a third finger, proud of my three caveats for a date with him.

Helios's smirk deepens, and he cups my chin. "Did I mention it's a bunch of former military men who fancy themselves snipers? Against just us."

Oh, talk dirty to me, sunboy. I school my face into a glare, though I can feel the excitement bubble inside me.

Helios pulls me into him, wrapping an arm around my waist. "Their opposition had to drop out at the last minute."

No doubt this is a tactic to get me to forget about my fun little rules. But he won't catch me out this time like he did before.

"Agree to my terms," I insist.

Helios's eyes sparkle. "I agree to two and three."

A win. I knew he would never agree to the first one. I would have been disappointed if he did.

"Fine," I grumble. "Deal."

Helios slams his lips to mine, leaving me breathless and dizzy as he murmurs against my lips, "You'd better get changed, kitten."

I bite his lip hard. "Don't tell me what to do."

Helios pulls back, spanking me sharply on the ass. "Hurry up."

I growl at him but disappear into my bedroom to change. I pull on some acid-wash mom jeans and a cropped knit sweater with a Ghostface mask on the front.

Helios is on his phone when I return to the living room. His brows pulled into a frown.

"Ready to go?" I ask.

When his eyes meet mine, he looks completely unburdened once again. He shoves his phone into his pocket, nodding at me. His eyes seem to brighten the longer he looks at me, but I brush past him on my way to the front door.

The crisp New York winter air barely registers against my skin. People gawk as they walk past Helios and me, wholly not dressed for the weather. Truthfully, this is nothing compared to how cold the nights occasionally get in Tartarus. Sometimes, it was so cold that my eyes froze open. It was painful and a bitch to heal.

Everyone talks about the fiery pits of hell, but no one seems to know about the glacial cold of the winter nights in the places where Hades' power is only present enough to hold the prisoners.

Helios takes my hand, and only from the contrast of temperatures do I finally feel how bitterly cold it is. I hiss at him, snarling softly, but Helios ignores me and whistles for a cab. Brakes screech as one comes to a halt in front of us, and Helios leads me to it, opening the door for me. I slide into the cab, and Helios follows, wrapping an arm around my back. He tells the driver our destination before kissing me softly. I try to resist the urge to kiss him back, but I can't, and instead, I deepen the kiss, moaning into his lips. But I pull back after a moment.

I pull back and lick my lips. "Hate you."

Helios chuckles, pulling me deeper into his side and nuzzling my cheek. "You won't be saying that when you see how awfully arrogant these mortals are."

I grin, the anticipation building.

The cab pulls to a stop. Helios pays and climbs out, offering his hand to me. I ignore it and slide out on my own. Sure enough, a team of fifteen meatheads is waiting in full blackout professional gear. I feel my smile turn wicked as they look at me, all smirking at just how easy it'll be to beat some pretty boy and his alternative-looking date.

"Hello, boys," I croon, practically purring. Helios laughs darkly, obviously also seeing what I see and how they are underestimating us.

One of them snorts, probably the leader, given how the rest of them look at him with a mixture of respect and admiration.

"I wonder how much you'll respect him when I destroy him," my madness chirps. It's not as present as usual and is quickly silenced as Helios cups my hip.

"Wow. They really scraped the bottom of the barrel to

take over the cancellation," the leader sneers.

Helios squeezes my hip, leaning down to whisper in my ear, "Told you."

I tilt my head, taking in each of them, cataloging them as future victims of my paintball tirade. A few of the men start to look a little uncertain as they take me in, but the majority stand comfortably in their smug arrogance.

The leader, and who I assume is his right-hand man, take a step toward me. "You lost, sweetheart?" he asks.

I feel my smirk deepen. "Always."

The right-hand man lets his gaze slide over me. "The babysitter's club is down the street."

"Oh, I know," I quip. "It's right next door to the small cock gentleman's club. I'm sure I've seen you hanging out around there multiple times."

Helios laughs, squeezing my hip again. "You know. I almost feel bad for the hell she's about to unleash upon you."

Another spike of thrill jolts through me from his words. The pride in his voice fills me with warmth.

I watch the men, and the ones that were uncertain before look more so now, and the others look furious about the insult to their obviously penile-impaired friend. The leader narrows his eyes at me and turns, leading his men to retrieve their weapons and then regrouping to make a plan. Helios hands me some goggles, and I grab one of the paintball guns.

"Ready to absolutely destroy some dicks?" Helios asks, grinning at me.

"Let's fucking do this."

Helios knocks his gun against mine. "I'll definitely get more of them than you."

"Please." I roll my eyes.

"Care to make a bet?" he asks.

Fucker had planned this, but I do love a bet.

I quirk a brow. "I'm listening."

Helios pulls me against him. "If I win, you are my girlfriend."

"And if I win?"

He raises a brow. "What do you want?"

I smile, crossing my arms. "You to go away forever."

He shakes his head, looking unconcerned. He obviously heard the lie in my voice. "Pick something else."

I think for a moment, and when it comes to me, my smile fades, and my heart pounds. It's such a vulnerable thing to ask for, and I already feel like every second I spend with Helios, he demands more vulnerability from me. But it is truly something I would love to have from him.

"You spend a night with me. In the Underworld," I say before I've truly decided to speak.

Helios scans my eyes for a moment and nods once. "Done."

At that moment, I am so very grateful for him. I swallow and internally brush myself off. "And you buy me tacos whenever I want them for three years," I add, trying to lighten the mood. However, this does mean that when I win, I'll need to keep him around for at least three years to take full advantage of the free tacos.

Helios smirks. "Fuck yeah."

I nod. "Okay. We have a bet."

Helios kisses me hard, his lips insistent and desperate against mine. He pulls back, his eyes dark but lit with the light of battle. "Let's crush some balls."

I pull back, grinning. "And then you fuck me in their blood!" I screech as I take off into the trees.

Chapter Twenty-Eight

Helios

AND THEN YOU FUCK ME IN THEIR BLOOD!" she shouts as she runs into the trees, her paintball gun ready. A couple of the attendants laugh after a moment, thinking she's joking. There is one who looks slightly alarmed, and I make sure to lock eyes with that man and wink, heading off after her.

I'm going to marry that girl. I race after her, following the sound of her manic laughter. The high-pitched scream of a mortal pierces the air, followed by a stream of curses.

"What the fuck?!" another mortal shouts, and without a doubt, I know it's directed at Melinoë. She invokes that kind of reaction in most people.

"Death to your micropenis!" she shouts like a battle cry, the sound reverberating through the woods.

I knew this would be a good date idea. It's too bad there aren't places we could go to hunt people for fun. Okay, that is a bit more deranged of a thought than I am used to, but it's a very Melinoë thought. She's definitely rubbing off on me in all the best ways.

I lift my gun and close one eye to aim, shooting two mortals in the back of the head. The rules say I am supposed to aim for their chests, but whatever. So what if they wake up with a huge knot and bruises on the back of their heads?

"I'm up two, baby!" I shout to Melinoë, knowing she'll hear me wherever she is in the forest.

Sure enough, I hear her cackle and say, "Slow ass fucker, I'm up seven!"

The only sound for the next few minutes is the trigger being pulled and various mortals cursing as I nail them.

It's a bit unfair to put a bunch of mortals against two gods, but who cares? I could listen to her insane laughter echo through the woods for days. It's better than any lullaby.

A paintball hits me in the middle of the back, and I whirl with the gun up, seeing Melinoë on the end of her gun less than ten feet from me. "Cheater!"

She laughs again. Paint is splattered over the side of her face, the white of her hair dappled with neon green, but she's practically glowing. Or she is until I shoot her in the boob.

"You're so dead, sunboy."

She vanishes, becoming one with the shadows beneath the trees. Okay, I have never seen her do that before. She uses shadows to travel, but there's a clear delineation between the shadows and her. This time, it was a seamless melding into the darkness. She tackles me less than ten seconds later, appearing from the darkness mid-air. Her limbs wrap around me, taking me to the ground. Even with the makeshift armor they provided for us to paintball in, the hit still made my bones rattle. She straddles my waist, keeping me pinned, the wild look back in her eyes. Wild but not lost, there's a stark difference between the two.

Wild is madness without the desolation. Wildness is something I can join her in.

"Hi, baby," I purr, looking up at her.

The bushes rustle near us, and she lifts her gun, her eyes still on mine as she pulls the trigger twice in quick succession. Based on the groans of pain, she hit her targets.

"I'm going to marry you one day," I groan, looking up at my wild hellcat with murder in her eyes. She moves the gun to my head. My eyes never leave hers as I whisper, "Do it."

I see uncertainty, vulnerability, and more than a touch of fear in her eyes. Even if she held a real gun, I would heal with no lasting effects. It's not that she worries about hurting me. It's the idea that I would let her do that to me, and it terrifies her that no matter what she does to make me run, I will still stay. My goddess doesn't know what to do with that.

Melinoë narrows her eyes at me, her gaze full of nightmares. She lifts the gun from my forehead and shoots the leader who's running at us. He curses as she nails her target, ending the game. She doesn't even check to see if he's down before she grabs my shirt in her fist and yanks me up to slam her lips over mine.

I lose myself in the kiss for a moment, nipping at her

lips. "We should go. Now."

She bites my lip. "You said you'd take me to dinner."

Fuck, who can even think about food right now? She rolls off me and pulls me to my feet, nearly dragging me back toward the road. Distantly, I hear someone call to remind us about turning in our gear, but I do not care at the moment. I prepare to flash us home, but she shakes her head at me, her eyes flashing with that same wildness again as she hails a taxi. I care even less when Melinoë pushes me into the cab and straddles me, rocking against me.

The driver keeps his gaze straight ahead, but I'm under no illusions that he isn't aware of what's happening. I whisper hoarsely into her ear, "How quiet can you be, baby?"

Without waiting for her answer, I weave an illusion over us for the driver. It looks like we're just making out in his back seat like a couple of teenagers when, in actuality, I'm tearing at my pants and shoving hers off. My illusions are far from perfect and nowhere close to what my father can do, but they will fool a mortal.

I pull her over me until she is straddling my lap again. Covering her mouth, I slam her down on my waiting cock, muffling her moans against my palm. I bite my cheek until it bleeds as she starts to ride me. Every jolt of the taxi only escalates the sensation of her rocking that soaking cunt on me, of the awareness of another person so close with no idea about the two gods fucking in his backseat.

Melinoë's eyes flicker with passion and uncontrollable lust, along with something deeper that she's too afraid to voice. I tighten my grip on her jaw and pull her toward me, replacing my hand with my lips. My hands grip her hips, my fingers leaving tiny bruises on her silky skin. Her little hands fist in my hair, crushing her mouth against mine, trying to muffle her shout as she comes. Her cunt convulses around my cock, stealing my own orgasm from me.

Melinoë rubs her cheek against mine, purring softly. I have grown addicted to that little hum her body does when she's truly content, my body shining brighter in response. I pant, not moving, not caring as the taxi continues in circles. The cabbie is giving us time, not wanting to interrupt the illusion of us making out, or he's running up his meter. With her in my arms like this, I don't give a fuck either way. I don't move until I see the cab driver glare at us several times in the mirror. I fix our clothes, putting us in position before letting the illusion drop. Melinoë shifts off my lap, and the cabbie immediately pulls to a stop outside the restaurant. Melinoë slides out of the cab, and I tip the driv-

er an extra three hundred dollars for the hassle. He grumbles as he takes it, muttering under his breath in Farsi. I snicker as I get out and take her hand.

She looks up at me. "Remember. The unhealthiest thing on the menu."

Despite the reminder, Melinoë orders surf and turf for herself and then a Caesar salad with light dressing for me. I was fully prepared for her to order me some sort of grease-laden concoction that would have my stomach tied in knots by the end, but she didn't. She ordered me a salad. When the food is served, I offer her a bite, but she hisses at me and lurches away dramatically. I laugh and pop the bite into my mouth, humming in pleasure.

"You're actually enjoying salad," she says, taking a big bite of her turf. "And they say I'm the psycho one just cause I have voices in my head."

I lower my fork. "I don't think you're psycho for hearing voices, and I don't think it's strange, either." Her lips linger on her fork, listening to what I'm saying. "I like to think you're never really alone when you have things to talk to."

She lowers her fork, glaring at me. "Eating rabbit food is weird, and we're never eating out again."

I smirk, leaning over to kiss her, keeping the conversation light as we finish our meals. The waitress returns with the bill and three massive steaks that Melinoë insisted she needed for Cerberus. She makes sure to add that she's talked to Berry about me, and the three-headed guard of the Underworld hates me as a result. Ah, the joys of being in love with the absolutely volatile Goddess of Nightmares.[9]

Chapter Twenty-Nine
Melinoë

HELIOS'S HAND WARMS MY LEG AS WE DRIVE THROUGH THE CITY. This trip is nothing like our journey to the restaurant. I contemplate pushing him away, but why bother? We both would see the lie of it. Plus, I like his hand on me. The warmth of his touch burns through my pants, which makes it feel like the barrier of denim does not exist. I squeeze the cold package of steaks for Berry to prevent myself from reaching out to Helios, focusing on the blur of colors as we travel through the city. There's a comfortable silence between us, and it crawls up my skin like an army of ants.

Why is comfort so foreign to me that it feels like an itchy sweater? I recognize I feel at peace, yet my body is tense and sharp.

The cab pulls to a stop, and it takes me a moment to recognize that we are outside my building. I don't even glance at Helios before I climb out, but he grabs my hand and slides out with me. I walk to the cab's open window and bend down, regarding the mustached cabbie. His round, ruddy face glares back at me.

"Give us a second. He has another stop." I say with a smile. I'm unsure what he sees in my smile, but the driver's irritated gaze melts away. He nods once and turns his attention to the road ahead, the car idling.

"Where am I going, hellcat?" Helios asks, smirking, his hand resting casually on the door.

"Home or wherever. I don't care," I reply, crossing my arms.

"Kicking me out before we've even walked into your building?" Helios loops his finger through my belt loop and pulls me closer.

"Yes. you are never welcome." I lift my chin, looking up at him and praying to the hells I'm not giving him any sort of bedroom eyes.

Helios laughs and kisses me softly. "Let's go, kitten."

Helios wraps his arm around my waist, and we step onto the sidewalk. He pushes the taxi door closed, and I smile into Helios's lips when I hear the driver curse, "Crazy fuckers." He revs his engine and shoots off down the street.

"You want me to leave?" Helios asks, dipping me.

"Yes," I lie, tunneling my fingers into his hair and holding onto him.

"Liar," Helios growls and deepens the kiss.

I yank his hair as he straightens with me and scoops me up into his arms, walking into my building and straight to the elevator. I blindly feel for the button to take us to my floor, my lips never leaving Helios's. The door opens on the wrong floor seven times before we reach our destination. Helios strides down the corridor, holding me and biting my lip. I can taste his need, and I am sinking into it when I feel his body suddenly go completely rigid.

"So this is what you've been doing," a cool feminine voice says.

Helios slowly puts me on my feet, the golden brown leeching from his skin.

"What are you doing here?" he asks, all kindness from his face and voice gone.

The intruder looks me over, and it strikes me how like Helios she is. The family resemblance is so obvious, but where he is the sun, she is the moon. Where he is warmth and light, she is eerie and cold. This must be Selene, then. The way she looks me over with such distaste is making my murderous instincts tingle.

"Can I talk to you alone, Helios?" Selene asks, looking down on me even though we are roughly the same height.

I growl softly at her, moving in closer to Helios like he's my cub and I'm a protective momma bear.

"Whatever you need to say, you can say in front of Melinoë," Helios says, wrapping an arm around my waist.

Selene narrows her eyes and snaps her gaze to Helios. "It's about the war, Brother."

Helios's body tenses, and I look up at him, seeing the unease on his face, the indecision. Of course, it had occurred to me that Helios would need to think carefully before pledging his allegiance to either the Titans or the Divine. But it hadn't occurred to me until right now how heartbreaking it would be for me if he chose wrong.

A moment passes, then another, and Helios still says nothing. The internal battle is clear on his face. I unwrap myself from him, feeling my guard starting to build little by little. Before this moment, I also hadn't realized how much he had broken through it.

Helios grabs my hand, interlinking our fingers, but keeps his gaze locked on his sister. "What more is there to talk about?"

I don't release his hand, but I do continue to watch him, trying to read him.

"Seriously?" Selene asks sharply, her words cutting through the tension like a serrated blade. "This is your fault," she hisses venomously at me. Only then do I focus on her. Selene's eyes are no longer eerie and cool. Now, there is an icy fire in them.

"Fuck off, Selene," Helios snarls, holding my hand tighter.

Selene blinks at him and then furiously storms away. She barges past us, leaving a chill in her wake. I tug my hand from Helios's, and he responds by growling and taking my hand again. I yank my hand away, and in a blink, I shadow away to the palace in the Underworld.

It doesn't take me long to find Cerberus. The big, sad lump is lying on his enormous navy bed in the kitchen. He doesn't even lift a head when I arrive. He simply opens one set of those large puppy dog eyes and sighs heavily. I'd be offended if this was how he always greeted me, but it's not. Berry and I have always been good friends. He's usually elated to see me. So elated that I feel guilty for my hatred of the realm, but today, the only person he wants to see is his mom, and I get it. She's the only person I want to see, too.

"Hi, Berry-boo." I sigh, walking to him and dropping the bloody package of steaks on the counter before climbing into the bed with him.

One of my favorite things about Persephone is her undeniable love for this beast. Even giving him a sickeningly cute nickname, which even Hades occasionally calls him. It suits him, even though he is a badass protector of the realm. When she's around, he's just an overgrown baby. Cerberus nuzzles his big, wet nose against my cheek, licking me once with his middle head.

"I'll let you get away with it this once because you're depressed. Next time, I'll have your tongues," I growl, but there's no threat in it, not really.

Cerberus huffs a laugh and lays his head down on me,

my face buried against his chest.

"Damn, this bed is comfy. Did Mommy buy it for you?" I ask, shifting slightly.

Cerberus whines softly in reply.

"What are you doing?" A soft growl from Berry follows Helios's voice, and I smirk with pride. I hear his footsteps get closer, and Cerberus growls louder, draping a heavy paw over me protectively.

"Kitten." I can hear his frustration in how he says my pet name.

I ignore him, nuzzling into Cerberus more. I bristle at the thought that Hades must have given Helios open access to the Underworld. That or he's too lost in his grief to care who comes and goes.

"Melinoë. Look at me," Helios growls, demanding.

He obviously takes a step closer because Cerberus growls louder, his chest vibrating against my face. Helios growls back, not backing down.

Hot.

"Baby. Talk to me. Look at me."

Cerberus barks at him, and the sound sends a shooting pain through my ear, thanks to our proximity. Cerberus stills, and I feel his body shiver. Something thumps wetly on the floor, and he scrambles up and bolts toward the sound. I glance over my shoulder to see Helios holding up another of the steaks I'd brought. After devouring the first one, Berry barrels to Helios and licks his face before snatching the second steak out of his hand.

I glare at Berry and then at Helios. "P will be pissed you didn't give a steak to each head." Not that it matters. They all feel the same thing. If one eats the steak, the other two will taste it. But Persephone always felt like she was being neglectful by favoring one head over another if they all didn't get one.

Helios tosses the final steak, the right head catching it easily and chewing happily as the other two heads watch Helios, their tongues lolling out of their mouths.

I try to glare at Cerberus again, who is a complete turncoat, but seeing the joy on his face for the first time since P was taken makes my heart swell. This happiness won't last, but seeing him enjoy the slightest glimmer of light, the burden of her absence leaving him for the slightest fraction of time warms my heart.

Helios offers me his hand, but I ignore it. I smack it away and slip out of the fluffy bed on my own, walking to the fridge, which is always stocked with the best stuff. I grab the first thing I lay my hand on and squeal in delight when I peel back the tinfoil, revealing a full apple pie.

The golden brown crust is the perfect balance of flaky and buttery. I pull a can of whipped cream from the fridge before kicking the door shut. Helios's eyes are fixed on me as I pop the lid off the whipped cream, the sound of the scoosh filling the room as I artfully cover the top of the pie. My eyes slide to Helios. He is still assessing me, his arms crossed across his chest.

I narrow my eyes at him and tilt my head back, squirting a large dollop of cream directly into my mouth before placing it to the side. I aggressively grab a fork and stab it into the pie, watching him as I take a bite.

"Baby."

I stab the pie again, taking another bite, glaring at him the entire time.

He glides to me, placing his hand over mine, stilling the fork as it hovers en route to my mouth.

"Words. Please."

I pull my gaze away from his, looking down at the pie. "You're taking their side."

Helios sighs, releasing my hand and leaning his hip against the island. "They're my family, Mel."

I don't look at him, I can't. I stab the fork into the pie, pushing it away a little. "Fine."

Helios cups my chin, angling my face up, forcing me to meet his gaze. "I'm torn. I—"

"I'm taking Cerberus for a walk," I interrupt, pushing him away and rounding the counter. At the word, Berry is already clamoring at the door, his paws heavily dancing against the marble.

"Okay," Helios says, and I hear the dejection in his voice.

I don't turn to look at him before grabbing Cerberus's blue and green ball launcher as we leave through the kitchen door. The grounds are vast, and from here, I can see Persephone's garden to the left. I try not to look at it, knowing it'll hurt. Then Berry will look, and he'll be sad, too. So I launch the ball for Cerberus. He chases it and brings it back, dropping it at my feet. Every time he returns, he barks impatiently, barely backing away enough for me to scoop up the ball again. But he bolts in anticipation once I have it, at least a hundred yards away before I've even raised it past my hip.

I feel Helios watching me the whole time, his eyes burning into me from the window. Eventually, I look over my shoulder at him, and something in his expression makes me want to go to war. It isn't quite pain, but it is something close, and I don't like it.

I lift my chin slightly, gesturing for him to join me. By the time he is striding across the lawn, an easy smile has replaced the look of uncertainty. He slides his hand into mine, but I yank away and thrust the ball launcher against his chest. Helios takes it but tips his head in question. "You'll need to work to stay in Berry's good graces."

Cerberus trots back, dropping the ball in front of him, but Helios just keeps watching me. "And your good graces? How do I get back into those?"

I roll my eyes. "You were never in them in the first place, asshole." I cross my arms over my chest.

Helios tugs my hand free, and Berry shuffles off, giving us a moment.

"Melinoë. No pretending for a minute."

I look up at him, unable to hide any of the vulnerability I can feel oozing from my pores.

"I love you," Helios says, interlinking our fingers. "You know, if it weren't for you, this choice would be easy. But you…" He searches my eyes. "You changed things for me."

I frown. "If it wasn't for me? What about Persephone?" They've been friends for years. He loves her, not romantically, but surely that means something, too.

Helios shakes his head. "Not even for P. They're…" He looks away. "They're my family, Mel. My sisters, my parents."

"But Hades protected you." My brows furrow more. What had his family ever done but cause him pain?

"You. Are. The. Only. Thing," he repeats, his gaze once again locked on mine. I force myself to look away, my mind reeling. He would choose the Titans over—

"I know it's ungrateful. I sound like an uncaring prick."

"You definitely do," I agree, pulling my hand from him.

Helios pauses for a moment, lowering his voice a little. "Persephone would save Hades over us. That's her family. I don't hate her for that."

I blink, looking at him, disbelieving. How could he possibly see that as the same thing? "That's her husband. Her fated mate. Her king."

"And you're mine."

"Stop." I bristle. "What have the Titans ever done for you, Helios?"

His flinch sends a dagger through my heart, but I don't back down or soften. "I had a life before the war."

I'm about to reply when I hear Berry whine. He's standing in Persephone's garden and dramatically collapses onto his stomach, surrounded by flowers. I look back at Helios, who still has his gaze trained on me. "We're not talking about this anymore. Do what you want," I growl, walking toward Berry.

"You don't care?" Helios asks, his voice devoid of his usual arrogance.

"No," I growl, the lie twisting my stomach.

"Right."

I lie down next to Berry and look up at the familiar granite-hued sky. Berry whines again, nuzzling one of the roses, the bloom swaying softly as he exhales against it. Helios lays down next to me, not touching me but close enough I can feel his warmth along my left side.

"I'm sorry, I don't have an answer."

"Thank you for being honest with me." The words slip out, a vulnerable truth that needed to be spoken.

"I'll always be honest with you." I feel the touch of his honeyed gaze. "Even when you're dishonest with yourself."

My heart speeds up in my chest, and the butterflies erupt in my stomach so hard it feels more like a murder of crows. I turn my head to look at him, and my breath catches when I meet his gaze.

"When you can't trust your own mind or thoughts. I'll always tell you the truth," he says.

I brush his pinky with mine and whisper, "I knew you were about to be mushy again. You just can't help yourself."

Helios leans in to brush his lips against my forehead, but I lift my chin at the last moment, snagging his lips with mine.

"Cerberus?" Hades calls out from the distance, his voice strained and broken.

I break the kiss and look toward the house. I see him standing on the balcony, his face wrecked, broken. He looks pale, thin, and destroyed. Even from here, I can taste his fear and sorrow. Cerberus nudges my cheek with his before he stands, whining as he runs toward Hades. Hades sits on the stairs, obviously not noticing us lying here in the dirt. Cerberus slows to a walk, nudging at his shoulder and whining again.

"I know. I miss her too." Hades' broken voice carries to us, and he presses his head against Cerberus's.

"I don't think he knows we're here," Helios whispers.

I nod, glancing at Helios for a second before I look back at Hades, my heart hurting for him.

"Fuck. We got this boy. We need to keep it safe for when

she comes back." Hades strokes Cerberus's neck again before he takes a breath and pulls back, his eyes red from tears. "Let's go, boy." He stands, and they both disappear back into the palace.

I watch them go, thinking about his pain, about my own. How would I feel if Helios had been taken? Would it even be the same situation?

"He's worse than I thought," Helios says, pulling me from my thoughts.

"He's… lost," I agree. "We should go."

"You have to dreamwalk him soon," Helios says, sliding his hand into mine.

I nod. "But he didn't see us here, so we should go and come back. That moment was not for us."

Helios cups my cheek. "Whatever you want, baby."

I shadow us back to my apartment and turn to face him.

"I'm going to fight," I say, looking up at him.

"Why?"

"Because they're my family."

Helios surprises me then by kissing me hard, cupping my cheeks. "I love you."

"Shut up," I growl as I kiss him back. Without breaking the kiss, I shadow myself back to the mortal world.[10]

I EASILY BREAK THE LOCK ON HER APART-MENT DOOR. I should be upset that she ran from me again, but it's a game we play. No one else understands. I doubt they ever could. Every time she runs from me, I know she's admitting to feeling more than she wants to feel for me. Every time she runs, it's a victory, another admission from her.

She left her bedroom light on, creating deep pockets of darkness in the living room. I wonder if she has caught on to my lack of night vision and left a single light on for me. Her silhouette cuts a slightly darker shadow that catches my eye.

"Baby?" I call softly as I move toward her.

"Hello again, sunboy," she purrs.

I close the distance. "You ran."

"You broke my door." She looks up at me, her eyes flashing but betraying a vulnerability that only shows in the shadows. "What do you want, Helios?"

I stroke her hair behind her ears, smirking as some of the dual-colored strands get caught on her piercings. She changes her earrings often, and I love that they never match. It means I am surprised every time I nip at her ears.

"The same thing I've always wanted," I say, not needing to elaborate.

She hisses, like the feral cat I always compare her to. I swear if she had fur, it would be sticking straight up right now. "Why can't you be normal and say you just want a good fuck?"

"Because it's been about more than a good fuck for me since I woke up alone on the bathroom floor of a club," I say.

Melinoë takes a step back, retreating from me ever so slightly, but it's enough to let me know how deep my words are sinking in right now. She snarls, continuing to back up until she hits the wall. I close the distance, but she puts her hands on my chest. Partially to stop me from getting any closer but also to keep me from retreating. Melinoë is more than duality in her hair and eyes. She is both fearless and fearful, brave and cowardly. Melinoë is nightmare and daydream.

"Helios. Stop," she whispers, but her fingers curl into my shirt.

I press my palms against the wall on either side of her head, caging her in. "No. I won't. Do not go where I cannot follow."

Melinoë gazes up at me, her eyes flashing with that same terror and vulnerability. She's never truly trusted anyone, not truly. She can't trust her own mind. How can she ever bring herself to trust another completely?

"Let me be the light that pierces your darkness, and when that doesn't work, let me hide in the darkness with you," I whisper huskily, brushing her hair back again.

She swallows audibly, and her hands drop from my chest, pressing her hands back into the wall. It is another retreat, something so visible, so tangible that I can almost feel her heart slamming against her ribs. I know that if I push more right now, she'll break. There is a fragile line I need to walk with Melinoë. It is a dance on the razor's edge of her mind. So, instead of pushing, I pull back.

"How about some food?" I ask, watching the way she visibly relaxes. It's a tiny truce, but it will do for now.

I nuzzle a kiss against her temple and ask, "Are you ready for another dreamwalk?"

They take a lot out of her, far more than she lets on. After I fed her full of tacos and we fucked last night, she passed out. I spent the time she was sleeping, cleaning her apartment a bit, fixing the lock, and, surprisingly, in contact with other Titans who had yet to declare for either side. Though some maintained extreme opinions about the Olympians, a few were hesitant to pick a side. Just like me.

She nods. "They're a little easier now."

"I'm going to be a little late, but I'll be there," I say, sliding my fingers up and down her arm.

She pulls back to look at me. "Does that mean you're actually going to leave me alone?"

I scrunch my nose, fake biting at her cheek. "Only for a bit. I'll be there before you put him under."

"Whatever."

Her tone betrays her, and I know she wants to ask me why. She wants to ask so many things, but she is too afraid it will appear relationshipy. One day, she'll come to realize that we are in a relationship. I could have sworn I heard her come close to saying love last night while we were fucking.

"I'm meeting up with my sisters," I say, feeling her tense next to me. "To decide."

It is time to flip the proverbial coin. Olympian or Titan. I know my decision will affect more than just my sisters and me. Other Titans are going to look to me now, too. I never thought of myself as having influence, but apparently I do.

"Don't care," she growls.

"Liar." I kiss her head and pull her back into me. "I'd invite you to come with me, but I figured your answer would be something around fuck and no."

She smirks at me, but doesn't pull away even as I press kisses over her face. "You're learning, sunboy."

I laugh. "Now, cry because I have to leave."

Melinoë ignores that, instead choosing to kiss me, digging her fingers into my hair. I groan into her mouth and pull her tighter against me. She wraps her legs around my waist, yanking me on top of her. She might not cry about me leaving, but she's upset about it all the same. I rock with her as she rubs herself against me, trying to entice me. Not that she truly has to try. I want to stay.

My fucking phone chooses this moment to ring.

Melinoë kisses down my neck, and I groan, reaching for my phone. "I have to go, baby."

She bites me, sucking hard on my neck, making my toes curl. A whimper escapes me even as my phone goes off again. Instead of trying to disentangle us, I stand, keeping her wrapped around me like a vine. She kisses me hard, biting my lip and yanking my hair.

"You keep kissing me like that, and I'm taking you with me," I growl into her mouth. She pulls back, her eyes scanning mine, silently looking for reassurance. I slowly lower her to her feet, pressing my forehead to hers. "I love you. I'll be there. I promise."

Melinoë stares up at me, her eyes betraying her. I kiss her one last time before I turn to leave. For a moment, the briefest of moments, I think I see her take a step to follow me, but the door closes, and I leave alone.[11]

---

11   The Queen & The King Chapters 24 - 34

Chapter Thirty-One
Melinoë

I FEEL IT BUILDING. The room is thick with it. His rage. His anguish. His desperation. The fear is irresistible, and it coats everything, viscous and thick. Hades' darkness fills the room, and the seductive call of the eternal void slicks my skin like jasmine-scented oil. It's different from before. This is more potent and penetrating. The feeling sinks into me, wrapping around my veins and polluting my blood. The voices sing in pleasure, reveling in my descent.

Helios is in front of me. I can just make out his form in the pitch black, but it feels like I'm watching a television program, not truly a participant in what is happening around me. His light dances against the edges of the darkness, but it's too late. I am already too far consumed.

Desire slithers through me, pooling at my core. My lips curl into a wicked smile as I willingly succumb to the prowling insanity clawing at me.

"Let's torture some assholes."

There is something so melodic about the sound of bones crunching, followed by the symphony of screams of pain. The warmth of blood as it splashes against my skin is delightful.

I swing my bat, slamming it into flesh and bone, savoring the feel of the different resistance depending on what I hit. Each sends a thrill down my spine.

There is no recognition, no consciousness here. It's just me, my bat, and the screeching inside my head. My vision splinters as I'm hit over the head, and I feel my chest rumble in laughter. The voices clang like bells, shrieking and murmuring wickedly. They circle my mind, passing my ears like the base of my skull is a drain.

I had given up trying to cling to the slightest awareness of my surroundings. Each time I got close to reality, I was pulled into the recesses of my mind. While things aren't completely black, the blood lust is controlling me, and I feel myself tumbling deeper and deeper.

I am lost.[12]

---

12   The Queen & The King Chapter 34

THE FORCE WITH WHICH I LAND INTO THE CELLS OF TARTARUS CAUSES A SOLAR BURST TO AROUND MY FEET, a flare of light flooding the darkness. My power shakes the walls and forces Hades out of the strange shadow form he'd assumed. Not that I care, fuck Hades. He can choke on his shadows.

Melinoë's laugh echoes off the adamantium walls, making me flinch. My eyes struggle to adjust to the dim lighting of the cells. She continues to laugh even as a Titan sinks his teeth into her thigh, drawing blood. I've heard her laugh in the throes of insanity, but this is different. Her normal laugh is like a struggling kitten fighting against a puppy determined to be its friend. This is… the sound someone makes when they've lost everything. It's the laugh of the hopeless.

I flash to her, searing the Titan attacking her with a concentrated beam. The focus takes effort when my power is raging, threatening to flood from me. I swing her into my arms, barely hearing the condemnation of the other Titans. They could all rot and take Hades with them. I lock my eyes on the God of the Underworld, and for a moment, I see the flicker of realization of what he's done. What he's made her do.

Too fucking late, asshole.

"She would be so disappointed in you," I hurl at him before flashing out of the Underworld and back to my flat.

I head straight for the bathroom and turn the shower on, adjusting the water, remembering how she used the cold water to comfort herself before. My breath hisses out of me as I step beneath the spray, the freezing water a shock to my system. I shiver, holding her tightly to me even as her body jerks, her eyes completely glazed. Her laugh continues, even more eerie with her vacant eyes.

"It's all right," I reassure her, even as the freezing water pelts us. I jostle her slightly to support her with one arm, kissing along the side of her face. "I know, baby. I know."

Something about my voice must penetrate the madness, but not in the way I'd hoped. Melinoë snaps and snarls before shadowing out of my arms. She reappears in front of me and summons a dagger of adamantium. Slamming me back against the wall of the shower, she holds it to my throat. Her eyes are still vacant, with no recognition of who I am, and an adamantium dagger could do serious damage, even scar me, but I don't move.

"Take me with you," I plead softly.

She hisses and presses the dagger harder against my throat for a moment before her shadows wrap around her, and she disappears. Fuck! Why didn't I cuff her? She doesn't know who I am. Of course, she would run! I'm such an idiot.

I warm my body to dry my clothes and flash to her apartment. Breaking the lock again, I storm inside, frowning when I find it empty. Where is she? For the next hour, I search every location I can think of. Hades' penthouse, Persephone's old apartment, the club we met, and even Plutus Industries.

When my search comes up empty, rage surges through me. This is all his fault. I flash back to the Underworld, finding Hades in the guest room he's been utilizing while Persephone has been gone. I close the distance and grab him by the collar. "Where is she?"

He shoves me away and adjusts his clothes. I stop, momentarily distracted. It looks like he is missing his hands, and the black tattoos have flooded his eyes. I shake my head, realizing I don't fucking care. I hope he loses his cock next.

"You've lost her?" he asks, tucking his handless wrists into his pockets as if that will stop me from seeing them.

My fist plows into his face, forcing him back a few steps. He doesn't even try to dodge. Of course, he would take all the joy out of hitting him. It doesn't stop me from hitting him again, just to be safe. This is probably the only time I'll get away with this.

"Where would she go?" I snarl.

His lip is split, but it's healing rapidly, faster than I've ever seen a god heal. This is his home realm. There is no satisfaction in this anymore, but I shove him again. He just looks at me. The way his dark tattoos are crawling up his body is even more alarming than Melinoë in the depth of her madness.

"Where it all began," he says simply.

My brows furrow. What the fuck does that mean? Where it all began? The look in his eyes shoots a chill down my spine, a shudder of foreboding. On impulse, I flash to the depths of Tartarus, where there is nothing but pure darkness. I press my hand to the jagged rock and start the treacherous descent. The cries of monsters best kept slumbering make me jolt, but I don't stop, refusing to let the oppressive darkness and the howls deter me. I'm looking for a very specific howling beast.

"Kitten?" I call.

A flicker of flame draws me deeper into the depths, a siren of light in the sea of darkness. The sound of scratching grows louder the closer I get to the fire. The entrance to a cave emerges from the darkness.

Scratch.

Fuck, what is that? I step inside and blink quickly, forcing my eyes to adjust to the light. A small fire crackles. The sound should be comforting, but it sends an ominous chill down my spine. Melinoë sits on the ground, rocking back and forth, her fingers clawing at the stone beneath her.

Scratch. Scratch.

"Kitten?" I whisper, approaching her slowly. Her hair is matted with dried blood, the white side stiff with gold, the black dusted with ash. She's muttering to herself as she continues to scratch. I drag my eyes down to her hands, and my stomach rolls when I see what she's done. There's nothing left of her fingertips but bone.

Scratch. Scratch. Scratch.

Is she even feeling this? She's farther gone than ever. Am I equipped to handle this? Fuck.

I stumble back and reach out to support myself against the wall. Sticky, warm wetness greets my palm. Tensing, I prepare myself for what I will see on the walls. It's blood. I know it is. The texture is familiar to me. I was a commander once, and I fought in the Great War. I would likely fight in another soon.

I thought I had braced myself, but I wasn't ready to see what was painted on the cave walls. Hidden in the depths of darkness from which Melinoë once sprang were countless images of… me.

Raising my palm, I summon a small sun to illuminate

the walls. My face looks back at me, over and over, painted in blood. Melinoë had captured me in all aspects of my emotions. Smiling, laughing, and in the throes of passion. Fuck, she'd even drawn me gagged and bound.

Melinoë snarls ferally, and my eyes snap back to her. She's drawing on the walls again, her skeletal fingertips covered in blood. "Must... find... Helios," she mumbles as she draws. "Helios... safe."

She's worried about me. That's kind of... sweet.

"Helios," I repeat softly, dosing the sun in my palm. "I can take you to him."

She pants raggedly, looking at me with wide eyes, but not truly seeing me, but she just gave me something to work with. There is one thing she seems to want, even in this state. She wants to make sure I am safe, and I can do that.

"I can take you to Helios," I say, my voice cajoling as I move closer, holding up my hands to show her I'm not a threat.

She glances at the paintings, tracing her skeletal finger along my cheek. "Helios... safe..."

I move closer. "I can take you to him," I say, watching the way her eyes flicker. My heart stutters, and I wonder if it's not about wanting to keep me safe. Am I safety to her?

She strokes the painting. "Helios..." Then, she vanishes.

Fuck. At least this time, I'm pretty sure I know where she's going. I flash back to my flat, hearing her in my bedroom. Following the noise, I find her in my closet. She's ripped all my clothes off the hangers and put them in a pile. Now, she is rolling around in them like a cat, searching for the comfort of their owner's scent. I carefully step closer and crouch at the very edge of the pile, not encroaching too far into her territory. She wiggles around until she has sufficiently buried herself before curling up into a tight ball. A moment later, I hear what sounds like exhausted snoring coming from her.

Fuck. Well, at least while she's asleep, I can tend to her wounds. Carefully, I wrap her bone fingers, seeing the slightest bit of muscle starting to regenerate. This is the awful part about our abilities. When we regrow limbs, it is layer by layer and extremely sensitive while in the process. I gently kiss the bandages before tucking her hands back against her. She jolts awake and looks up at me. I freeze, ready for her to vanish, but she lifts her hand and cups my cheek.

"I love you," she whispers.

I'm too stunned to say anything, surprised that she's even awake. Before I can respond, she passes out again. I stroke a matted lock of hair away from her face, a tear sliding down my cheek.

"I know, baby. I know you do."

I'll be your shelter, Melinoë.

Chapter Thirty-Three
Melinoë

MY HEAD IS POUNDING, MY BONES ARE THROBBING, MY FINGERS…

Fuck, my fingers are agony. I stretch them slightly, wincing at the pain I feel when I straighten them, the muscles taut.

"Careful, baby," Helios murmurs into my hair.

I groan softly as I slowly come to. I'm surrounded by his scent, his warmth enveloping me in that delectable way it does. It takes me a moment to realize that my whole body is shaking down to my bones. Helios gently pulls me closer, his temperature rising even more.

"Shhh, it's okay. I'm here," he whispers, kissing my head.

Why is everything so painful?

A memory shoots through my mind like a comet striking the Earth. I'm holding a bat, slamming it against the skull of a Titan, brains leaking from the fracture.

Fuck.

"How bad was it?" My voice is hoarse, like I've been screaming nonstop for hours, and it's finally succumbed to the strain.

I feel the tension in Helios's body as he strokes my hair comfortingly. "We don't need to talk about it."

I grimace. Obviously, it was bad enough that he isn't going to tease me about it. I crack open my eyes, pain radiating through my head at even the tiny bit of light.

"So very," I croak. I try to bend my fingers again, a whimper curling in my throat as pain shoots down my hand and into my wrist. It's an effort not to look at the damage I inflicted upon myself when I was in my state of insanity. No doubt I have been in worse shape, but it still isn't pleasant to see, and it's a bitch to heal in my weakened state.

"Are you…" Helios hesitates, his hand pausing as he strokes my hair. "Are you back?"

I close my eyes again, my heart sinking. Very, very bad.

"I am," I whisper, too cowardly to look up at him, to meet his gaze.

Helios cups my chin, angling my head up. I keep my eyes closed, afraid of what I'll see in his eyes as he looks back at me. "Hey." He slides his thumb along my jaw, and I finally find the courage to blink my eyes open. But when I meet his gaze, there is no shame there, no disappointment, no anger, and no pity. I only see concern, only affection, only… love.

"Stay with me." Helios's words are barely a whisper as he looks down at me, his golden eyes soft like honey, vulnerable, open, and unafraid.

Slowly, he leans in, allowing me plenty of time to pull away, to take space if I need it. But I don't. My breath hitches as his lips brush over mine, and I whimper softly at the gentleness. I look up at him, captivated by him.

"I'm here, Melinoë," he whispers, stroking his thumb along my jaw again.

I brush the tips of my fingers along his cheek, and he exhales, closing his eyes. "You went there without me."

I glide my fingertips along his jaw.

"You… you promised not to do that," he whispers, his voice breaking.

"I'm sorry," I whisper back, the apology sincere and true.

Helios covers my lips with his fingers, opening his eyes. "You never apologize for the monsters in your head."

My vision blurs as my eyes fill with tears, one slipping free and trailing down my cheek. I have never been so vulnerable with anyone, never let anyone see any weakness, but I don't care. These tears are for Helios. They are tears of despair that I descended. They are tears of gratitude that he found and cared for me. They are even tears of growing, undeniable feelings.

Helios wipes the tear away. "I love your monsters. I love your darkness. They are part of you. You never have to apologize for them."

I search his eyes, feeling another tear slip free. I lean in and kiss him deeply, the salty droplet flavoring our lips.

I tunnel my fingers into his hair but pull back with a wince as I extend my fingers. I focus on my wrapped hands, and Helios follows my gaze. He takes my hand in his and caresses the bandages.

"They'll be fine in a few hours," he says, kissing the back of my hand.

I nod. The memory of the sound of bone against stone makes the hair stand on the back of my neck, and I force it away.

I lie back, noticing that we're not in his bed as I'd thought. Instead, we're lying on the floor in a pile of his clothes. I'm about to question it when Helios kisses me again, stealing my breath and my thoughts.

"Safe," I moan into his lips, deepening the kiss. He moves on top of me, his whole body so warm and comforting.

Helios bites my lower lip, gently pinning my wrists above my head so I can't accidentally hurt my healing fingers while they're still so fragile. I slide my knees along his hips and once again marvel at how easily he fits against me. His hips nestle between my thighs like the last piece of a jigsaw puzzle. He pulls back after a moment, looking down at me with the intensity of all the suns in the universe.

"I love you. Demons and all."

I just stare up at him, not hiding from the immensity of his words, of his stare.

Helios presses his forehead to mine. "Next time you find yourself staring at the darkness in your head, you take me with you. Okay?"

A third tear falls as I nod, closing my eyes. Helios kisses the tear away. "You are not alone, Mellie, even in the fight in your head. I am there with you. Always."

"I love you, Helios." The words come out as easily as a breath, and they're quiet, so quiet, yet the enormity of them swarms through me. Helios doesn't immediately reply, and I open my eyes after a moment. His glow singes my retinas, but I don't look away.

"I love you too," he replies, his voice full of emotion.

"Kiss me," I practically beg, and it's less than a moment before his lips descend on mine eagerly. He moves my wrists to hold them both with one hand and uses his other hand to cup the back of my thigh, pulling it higher on his hip. His warmth covers me, every part of my body pressed against it. I arch, needing to be even closer to him. It feels as though it's seeping into me, sinking through my skin, pushing the darkness back even farther. His warmth, his light filling me.

"Inside me…" I moan, needing to feel even more full of him. Helios burns our clothes off, and without pausing, he buries himself inside me.

I lift my hips, moaning into his lips as he starts to thrust into me, but the moments aren't hurried and frantic like usual. This is slow and intimate, our bodies anchored to one another, holding each other there.

Helios groans, panting into my mouth as he continues his maddening ministrations with his hips, his kisses deep and passionate. "I love you."

I tug against his grip, wanting to touch him even knowing I can't right now. I roll my hips beneath him, taking him even deeper.

The intimacy and love are heavy around us, and we both lean into it, craving it. I've never been like this with anyone before. I've never felt so connected, safe, or accepted, and the feeling makes my core throb.

"I'm here," Helios whispers into my lips.

My pussy pulses, getting wetter as I near my release, but Helios keeps up the steady pace, his body rocking against mine. With every brush of his skin against mine, electricity seems to spark beneath my skin.

"I love you," Helios repeats. "And your demons, not despite them."

I deepen the kiss, his lips muffling my cries of pleasure as I find my orgasm, the world splintering around me. Helios roars into my mouth, finding his own release and filling me with his heat. My whole body relaxes beneath his, and he finally releases my wrists, dragging his lips along my cheek. Within moments, the world fades to black again, comforted by his weight and warmth on top of me. I know I am safe. I am with Helios.[13]

Chapter Thirty-Four
Melinoë

I WATCH THE CURSOR FLASH ON MY PHONE, considering how I want to reply to him. It's not that I'm mad at Hades. I can see his struggle. Part of what pulled me into my insanity was that I could feel his struggle.

Helios tenses next to me, his fingers stilling in my black hair. Has he been reading my messages over my shoulder? Nosey fucker.

"He can't be serious," Helios growls, his chest vibrating slightly beneath my head where it rests on him. "He expects you to dreamwalk him again? After what he did?"

I frown, still looking down at my phone. "Hades didn't do anything." I sigh, unsure why I'm defending the God of the Dead. My inner voice, the true one, not one of the plaguing voices, but the one that speaks to me with only logic and kindness, whispers that he needs someone on his side at the moment. And that someone is me. I also find a great deal of comfort in knowing it's what Persephone would want, which helps push away the nagging feeling of hopelessness. I'm helping in some way, however small.

Helios growls again, "Yes, he did."

I lift my chin, looking up at him. "He didn't."

Helios squeezes me, pulling me even tighter against him. "He deliberately provoked your insanity. Then he took you to torture Titans."

"He's just…" I look away, playing with one of his shirt buttons. "He's going through a rough time."

"Bullshit," Helios snarls, snapping his teeth. "Don't make excuses for him."

His anger surprises me, and I feel his whole body thrum under it. There's something sexy about his anger and his reasons for getting angry. He wants to protect me.

Even still, I push back. "I am always on the edge, Helios." The need to defend Hades at this moment is overwhelming.

Maybe I'm going soft.

I'm definitely feeling more mushy today. It's like my usual solid, fiery core is molten and gooey. It's truly awful and definitely a temporary side effect of plummeting from the brink. The memory of telling Helios how I felt about him yesterday makes me cringe, but then I remember the look of pure joy on his face, and it melts it into nothing.

Definitely going soft.

Helios relaxes beneath me, cupping my chin and lifting it so I look up at him again. I try not to think about how easily my body molded against his when we lay down like this. His intense caramel gaze covers mine, making me acutely aware of every single fucking place our bodies touch, which, in this position, is almost everywhere.

"It is your edge to walk, Mel. He is not allowed to push you over." His honeyed voice trickles along my skin with such warmth.

"He needs this, Helios," I reply, though it comes out as mostly a moan. "He needs Persephone." We all do.

Helios growls softly again, stroking my hair back. "And I need you."

My lips tug into a stupid smile, but I force out a groan of contempt. "Gods, you're so embarrassing," I say, grabbing his face and slamming my lips to his, moaning when he immediately opens for me.

Too soon he pulls away, and I search for his lips again with mine, but instead of kissing me, he presses his forehead to mine. "Your sanity is not something for him to play with. If you fall over the edge, it's because of you. No one else," he whispers breathlessly. "And I'll follow if you do."

I pull back, searching his face. "He wasn't playing with it."

"Mellie, he knew what he was doing."

I sigh. "Did he encourage me a little? Sure. But it was

my fault."

Helios strokes my cheek so tenderly that my heart aches in a way it never has before. "How?"

"Because I—" I pause, the truth roiling through me. "Because I wanted to do it. I didn't mean to plunge into myself, but I wanted to… torture."

Helios narrows his eyes, growling, "If you wanted to torture some assholes, that's fine. But I don't like how it happened, that he pushed you to the brink and hasn't even apologized."

"You think his head is on anything other than getting his wife back right now?"

"I don't care. Not if the cost of his actions is at the expense of your safety. Of your sanity," he continues.

"Safety?" I ask, lifting an eyebrow.

Helios blinks. "Did you see your fingers?"

I wince, stretching out my now completely healed fingers, the phantom aches throbbing dully in the joints. I sigh, sitting up and climbing out of bed, moving to look at my reflection in the mirror.

"This isn't about what happened before." I glance at Helios in the mirror. He's now sitting up, leaning back on his elbows. "This is about your beef with Hades."

Helios meets my gaze in the mirror. "It is about what happened." He sits up more, shifting to the edge of the bed. "Because I don't think he appreciates what you're putting on the line for him."

I pick up a cotton pad, apply some toner, and swipe it over my cheek. "So what? I should take away the one way he can speak to his wife?" I ask.

Helios simply sighs heavily and stands up, my gaze moving over his reflection appreciatively. He walks up behind me and squeezes my shoulders. "You are my priority, kitten."

I look up at him over my shoulder. "Okay, so reverse the roles. What would you do if you were in his position?"

From the way his eyes flash, I can tell I've won this round with just that one question. "He could rein it in a little," he growls, glaring down at me, though I know his irritation is not directed at me, not really.

"Would you?" I ask, trying to stop my chest from puffing with pride at the impact of my questions.

He sighs, and his eyes soften as he cups my chin. "Why do you have to make such good points?"

I just smirk back at him.

"Don't look so proud of yourself," he growls, but this

one is playful, content, and mollified.

I wink up at him. "Can't."

Helios's lips tug into that maddeningly boyish smirk, and he bends, biting my neck when I turn my attention back to the mirror. My gaze never lands on myself, always locked on the blond Titan and the way his skin glows as he inhales me.

MELINOË AND I TRAVEL TO THE UNDER-WORLD TOGETHER THIS TIME, HEAD-ING DIRECTLY FOR HADES' STUDY. The venerable God of the Underworld looks completely broken. He seems so… defeated, and my lingering ire lessens slightly but not completely because he's still a dick.

"You came," he breathes out in relief. His voice is strained, the bags under his eyes visible even under those alarming tattoos he's clearly trying to hide under his glamour. Still. A. Dick.

"Of course, I came, demon daddy," Melinoë says. "I'm worried about P."

Worried about P. It's an understatement, but my gut twists at how Melinoë doesn't mention what happened last time, how Hades exploited her mental state for his selfish need to exact punishment on someone. Maybe my ire hadn't eased as much as I'd thought.

Hades focuses on Melinoë, his normally clear and shrewd eyes clouded with everything going on. But for a moment, there's a spark of something in his gaze that looks almost like the old Hades. "I lost control and dragged you with me."

"That will never happen again," I snap, my back straight as a rod.

Yeah, I don't care that the last time we faced off, he let me kick his ass. I remember the Titan war… or the one before the current one. Hades' shadows had collared my throat, pinning me to the ground as Hera put her hand through my chest, ripping my still-beating heart from it. I know the God of the Underworld's power firsthand. But I still don't give a fuck about that right now.

Melinoë brushes past me and picks up the solid gold globe from Hades' desk. Tossing it into the air, she catches it over and over. "It's fine. Is Morphie here?"

Hades watches Melinoë, not looking at the globe, but he eventually snatches it out of the air. I muffle a gasp when I see his hands. They're exposed muscle and bone. I'd noticed his missing hands the last time we fought, but they should have regrown by now. Which means he's lost them again. A shudder of foreboding shoots down my spine. He's made a deal, and it is costing him dearly. I close my eyes for a second and inhale deeply. There's the slightest trace of roses in the air. Persephone? Has Hades seen her recently? If he has, why hasn't he mentioned it? Why does he still look like an absolute mess? Something is definitely going on. He's acting odd, and more odd than he has been.

"Not yet. I wasn't sure if you'd come." He places the gold globe back down precisely before hiding his hands again. My eyes catch on the globe's new stand. Are those… hands? Two hands that do not belong to Hades are supporting the golden globe.

Oh fuck. That's why he's losing his hands. He made a deal with Nem. Oh fuck. He's really off the deep end.

"Have I ever let you down?" she asks, the implication clear in her words, vibrating around the room. Unlike you.

He flushes, rightfully so, and nods. "Let's go."

My eyes drift to Melinoë, trying to read her face, but she deliberately keeps her eyes averted from mine. She's catching onto my ability to read her thoughts through her eyes. Nice try, kitten. If I can't read your face, I'll find another way.

I trail them as they head for the spare room where I know Hades has been sleeping. The pathetic fool can't even look at the bedroom he shared with Persephone. I wonder what I would be like in his shoes. I wouldn't be a little bitch like him, that's for sure.

Morpheus waits patiently for us in the spare bedroom, his hands clasped in front of him. He doesn't even flinch at Hades' haggard appearance. The God of Dreams obviously knows about Hades' spiral.

"What do you mean you can't find her dream, Morphy?" Melinoë demands. The God of Dreams hovers over Hades in the bed, prepared to drop them into an apparently non-existent dream.

"It's as if she's… gone."

Hades snarls, the sound more feral and monstrous than ever. His shadows erupt, slamming into both Melinoë and Morpheus. She flies back, hitting the wall hard enough to crack it. Morpheus slams into a table, snapping his teeth and biting back his retort.

"Throw my girlfriend one more time, and we will have issues," I warn, narrowing my eyes on him. I move to help her to her feet.

"I'm not your fucking girlfriend," Mellie hisses, slapping my hand away and standing on her own. "Hades. You need to calm the fuck down. We're doing all we can here."

He jumps to his feet, his glamor failing. I gasp at seeing the swirling tattoos that cover every inch of his skin. There's even more than before. They're covering his horns and wings, moving around insidiously.

"Yet, it is not enough! We are at war, and my queen is trapped!"

"Are you fucking kidding me?" Melinoë snarls. "I have been nearly killing myself to ensure you can see her as often as you want, and you have the fucking nerve to tell me it's not enough?"

"Is she here right now?"

"No, and neither am I!" She whirls, shouting, "Berry! Come!"

Cerberus trots to her side.

"You must not truly care about her." Hades snarls the venomous words at her, and she flinches.

That's it.

Hades' breath whistles out of him as I slam into him with the force of a comet. We hit the window, breaking the glass. His wings snap out to stop him from plummeting into the gardens below, but at this point, I hope he falls.

"You may be a king, but you don't have to be a dick," I growl, my eyes glowing.

Mellie doesn't look back, taking Cerberus on a walk with her, leaving us alone. Morpheus must have taken the opportunity to vanish.

"Question my loyalty all you want." I glare at him, spitting the words. "Because, yeah, I haven't always been on your side."

"And now?" he hisses, his eyes narrowed. Fuck, they are obsessed with this. Why does my loyalty matter so much?

I slowly rake my eyes over him. "I'm not going to answer that because my loyalty isn't important, but Mellie's loyalty? To question that? You and Persephone are her family. She would do anything for you!" Hades' jaw audibly cracks, but I don't stop. "And let me tell you this. P was my friend first, so yeah, I hate this. I hate that this cold bitch has a hold of her. But I know of all people, even without her memories, Persephone never needed saving. Anyone who crosses her is put into the ground or worse. So get your head out of your ass."

I spin on my heel, leaving the prick alone, surrounded by broken glass.

Still. A. Dick. [14]

Chapter Thirty-Six
Melinoë

THE ROOM REEKS OF DESPERATION AND PAIN. I watch Hades. He's not even sensed me here, too lost in himself to even be aware of his surroundings. The faint smell of roses still permeates the air, not the pure smell of freshly cut ones, but the one that emanates from Persephone. He's seen her recently, and for whatever reason, it has soured his mood more than improved it. I wonder if it's got something to do with the hint of iron that mingles with her scent. She was hurt. Badly. The thought sends a searing rage through me, but I keep my gaze locked on Hades.

His wings and horns are obsidian, thanks to the roiling darkness within him. Soon, Persephone won't have a husband to return to unless he gets control of it. The voices croon in my head, desperate to feed from his pain, but I push them away, focusing on my friend.

Hades turns, meeting my gaze, and his body tenses.

"Pull yourself together." My voice is sharper than I mean it to be.

Hades laughs sadly, moving past me, the glamour shutting away his dark wings and horns.

I don't move from my position, leaning against the door, but I track him as he crosses the room. No part of this space is similar to his and Persephone's bedroom. It's fairly bland, perfect for a guest room, but it feels lifeless, probably the same way Hades feels. The bed sheets are still rumpled from whenever he was last in it, a pale pink silk negligee peeking out from beneath the other pillow.

He stalks toward one of the two armchairs, even his footsteps conveying his hopelessness. I push off the door, pour two very heavy-handed measures of the most expensive-looking scotch, and hand him one of the crystal tumblers before curling up in the other armchair. The fireplace crackles warmly in front of us, sparking every so often.

"I'm really losing it," Hades whispers so softly I almost miss it.

I take a long drink. The warmth from the fire coating my skin feels foreign now that I've become so accustomed to Helios's warmth.

"Persephone is being so strong." I look down at the amber liquid swaying in my tumbler. "So wherever your control is, I suggest you find it because she'll be pissed when she finally comes back to us and you're batshit."

I glance at Hades, who is still studying his drink like it holds all the answers. "Zeus wants Helios." His sapphire blue gaze swings to me, steelier than I've ever seen it. "In chains," he adds.

Anger and fear lick beneath my skin, my body trembling. The glass shatters in my hand, shards embedding in my palm and fingers. The newly healed skin is exquisitely sensitive, but I barely feel or acknowledge it.

"What." That is all I can say. It's not a question but a demand for answers.

Hades' voice is just as icy as his stare. "He wants to bring in Helios's father and his two sisters, using him as bait."

I snarl. The memory of the aftermath of Helios's last encounter with Zeus fuels my rage, and I'm vaguely aware of Hades asking me a question. His careful gaze locks on mine, but all I hear is my blood surging through my body. I try to sort through my thoughts, making a plan.

I grab the untouched tumbler from his hand, downing it in one long drink. "I have to go, but I'll be back tomorrow." Without waiting for a response, I shadow back to the mortal realm and Helios's place.

Zeus is missing and suspected to be captured, but that could be a ruse. It also doesn't guarantee Helios's safety. He has so many people at his disposal to do his bidding. If anything, this makes the situation more dangerous. There is no way to track his movements at the moment. He could be anywhere.

The apartment is in complete darkness.

"Helios?" I call, but there is no reply. I frown, quickly checking the rooms. I'm about to call him when I realize he's probably at my place. Hastily, I grab a collection of his clothes and stuff them into one of his brown leather duffle bags.

I tell myself not to worry until I have to and shadow to my apartment. "Helios?" I internally exhale when I see him sitting on the couch, perfectly at ease.

"Hi, kitten," he says, looking up at me, his lips pulled into a crooked smile. "I figured you wanted some alone time."

I practically run to him. "We have to go." I take his hand, trying to haul him off the couch, but he just looks at my hand wrapped around his, blinking uselessly.

"Go?" he asks, perplexed.

I yank his hand again, trying to pull him up. "Come on," I urge him. While Hades never gave a time limit for Helios's safety, I imagine that Zeus will come after him as soon as possible.

Helios frowns, moving at a snail's pace. "Why?"

"I'll explain everything later. I packed you a bag. We have to go. Now."

Helios finally stands, cupping my cheek. "A bag?" He looks so confused.

I yank his hand again, pulling away from him, knowing if I start moving, he will follow. "Come."

"Hellcat, talk to me," he says, trailing after me as I charge around my apartment, grabbing things to pack. I have a full wardrobe of clothes in the Underworld, but I make sure to grab the other things I may need: weapons, my journal, some books on dreamwalking.

"Melinoë," Helios growls.

I stop and look up at him. "I'll explain everything, but you need to come with me. Okay?"

Helios scans my eyes and nods after a moment. "Let's go."

I exhale in gratitude and move into him, wrapping us both in shadows as I take him to the Underworld.

My bedroom hasn't been touched since the last time I was in it. The walls are still dark purple with black crown molding. The black wood flooring is covered by a large purple shag rug with little white ghosts dancing around the border. I walk to the bed and drop the bags, wrinkling the formerly crisp black sheets. The black gossamer curtains hanging from the large gothic bed frame billow lightly in a non-existent breeze.

I wish I could love this room. I wish I could feel safe in it. Hades gave me complete creative control when decorating it for that reason. He wanted this to be a home for me, but it never has been. It's not Hades' fault. It's just because of my past in this realm.

"The Underworld?" Helios muses, looking around the room.

I nod, walking to open the patio doors to my balcony, allowing in some of the crisp Underworld air. The silver moon casts an eerie glow over the vast planes of the realm. It would be beautiful if I weren't so well-versed in the horrors that existed out there.

Helios leans against the railing, his eyes on me. "Melinoë."

I continue to look out at my home, my realm. My scars ache as they do whenever I return here. "It's the only place you're safe."

Helios covers my hand on the metal of the railing. "Safe?"

I don't move, don't reply.

"You don't like being here," he says.

I shrug. "If it keeps you safe," I look at him, "then it's my favorite fucking place in all the realms."

Helios shifts closes, wrapping an arm around my waist and tugging me against him. "Keeping me safe from who?"

"Who do you think?" I ask, looking up at the moon.

"My family?" he asks, his thumb stroking over my hip.

"Zeus."

When Helios doesn't reply, I look at him again, his gaze locked on me.

"Oh."

I turn to face him fully, and he pulls me into him, his warmth immediately enveloping me.

"You brought me here, even though you hate it," he cups my cheek, "to keep me safe?"

I roll my eyes. "Don't make a big deal about it."

Helios doesn't quip back at me. He simply leans in and presses his brow to mine.

I close my eyes and brush my nose against his. "Promise me you'll stay," I say, my voice barely a whisper.

"You'll be here?"

I nod, and he nods too. My whole body relaxes at that

promise, so much so that I don't even care if I'm being vulnerable, embarrassing, or mushy. I just feel so fucking relieved that he is here and he is safe.

Although, of course, for good measure, I say wryly, "Don't take this to mean that I like you or whatever. Gross." I cross my arms, glaring at him, though my lips curl into a smile.

Helios smirks. "Wouldn't dream of it."

"Good boy."

Helios growls and looks out at the Underworld and its raw, untouched beauty.

I push off the railing and head back into my room. Plopping down on the bed, I pull out my phone and open my messages with Persephone.

MELLIE

Your brother-in-law is the W O R S T. I cannot stress enough how much I hate him. Given how big an arrogant fuckturd he is, he must have the tiniest cock on all the realms. Poor Hera…Anyway, Helios is staying in the Underworld for a few days thanks to your dick brain of a brother-in-law. I guess he can just stay in my room with me. Wouldn't want to put you out or anything. But you definitely owe me one. Love you, P.

"Who are you texting?"

My head snaps up just as I press send, and I see Helios closing the patio doors.

"My boyfriend," I reply, smirking.

Helios quirks a brow, pulling out his phone and scrolling through it. "Liar."

I narrow my eyes at him. "You are not my boyfriend."

Helios walks over, bending to kiss me deeply. "Whatever you say, hellcat."

I sink into the kiss for a moment before pulling back, my hands braced behind me on the bed.

"What?" Helios frowns down at me.

"I've… never slept here," I admit, my stomach churning with the admission, the vulnerability. Sure, I've spent the night in the palace, maybe drifted off on a couch, but never in this bed, and I've never truly slept.

Helios tilts his head, his golden eyes that always see too much peering into my soul. "I promised you a sleepover in the Underworld."

"You did."

He smiles. "Looks like I'm about to fulfill that."

"Shower with me first?" I don't know why I'm nervous asking the question. We've been together so many times, yet just being here feels like a whole other situation. It feels like more.

Helios nods and straightens to allow me up.

On the way to my bathroom, I disrobe, discarding clothes as I go, throwing them haphazardly to the side. I feel Helios's molten gaze roams over my skin. The color scheme of the bathroom follows, but while the bedroom is plush and cozy, this room is covered in dark tile. It's modern and sleek but still homey to me.

I step into the shower and turn it on, the water running hot. It sluices over my skin, and my muscles practically groan in relief. Obviously, I was more tense than I thought.

Helios slides in behind me, wrapping his hands around my waist and leaning down to kiss my neck. I tilt my head for him, moaning as my core pools with desire and pleasure. He nips at the delicate skin of my throat, the small bite of pain making my toes curl ever so slightly. Everything feels more potent in the Underworld, probably because this is where I'm strongest. Helios's tongue laps over the mark he's left, soothing the sting but leaving a scalding trail of pleasure in his wake. His teeth tug at my earlobe, and I reach behind me, tunneling my fingers into his hair.

"Spread your legs for me and purr," he growls into my ear, and the sound has me tightening my fingers in his hair.

"Don't tell me what to do," I growl back, but my traitorous body instinctively obeys him.

Helios presses his palm against my stomach, pulling my back against him. His achingly hard cock presses against my ass, and the contact elicits the most painfully delicious moan from him. I rock my hips against him, feeling the steely heat of him slide against me like a brand. He dips his hand lower, his fingers brushing lightly over my pussy. I arch my back, pushing my ass back into him. He curses, low and filthy, before pressing my face against the shower wall and thrusting inside me hard. I brace my hands on either side of my head, moaning at the pleasure, at the bittersweet agony of that first thrust before my pussy has time to adjust to his size.

"Fuck."

Helios digs his fingers into my hips as he forges into me, hard and fast. He trails one of his hands up my torso, his fingertips searingly hot against my skin, and pinches my nipple. I arch at the feeling of his blisteringly hot touch against my sensitive breasts.

"Fuck. So wet for me," he growls, his hips unrelenting.

My nipple tightens beneath his fingers, making the pleasure even more exquisite, and I arch my back, desperate for more of him, for everything.

He bites my shoulder hard, and I cry out for him. My arousal spills out of me as he thrusts, his rhythm steady, hard, and deep. Helios moves his other hand from my hip, giving my other nipple the same treatment. It's already hard and waiting, anticipating the sweet fucking agony of it. He pinches both nipples, his grip an exquisite agony that sends me over the edge. I come, shattering into a million pieces, and the world as I know it collapses around me.

Helios groans and pulls out of me despite my body's attempts to hold on to him. He spins me and grips my thighs, lifting me off my feet before plunging back inside me, his cock forcing its way into my swollen and still quivering cunt. I slam my lips to his, my whole body trembling with aftershocks. I am lost to the way he works my body, focused on my pleasure. His tongue flicks against mine as he pounds into me, his skin slapping against mine.

I pull back and pant out, "Helios. Take me to our bed."

Helios's hips slow. "O-our bed?"

I nod, sliding my tongue along his lower lip. He immediately follows my instructions, carrying me out of the bathroom, his cock still buried inside me. We land on the bed, both of us still soaked from the shower, but I don't care. Helios looks down at me, his hips still unmoving.

"I love you," he says, cupping my cheek tenderly.

"Helios… Fuck me," I groan. "I need you to cum. I need it inside me, and I need it in our bed," I continue when he doesn't move.

He moans, the sound so guttural it is nearly feral, but he starts moving again, his hips snapping into me. I drag my nails down his back, breaking the skin, loving how he shudders and snaps his hips hard against me, his cock slamming so deep it takes my breath away.

"You're so fucking tight, kitten," he growls in my ear.

"Don't stop." I rock my hips in time with his thrusts, working him deeper.

Helios looks down at my breasts, his gaze caressing the marks he's left there. He groans at the sight. "Fuck, I like marking you."

I arch beneath him. "Of course you do, you obsessive asshole."

He smirks. "Do you hate it? I guess I shouldn't do it again."

I snarl. "Don't you fucking dare stop."

"You love it."

"No."

"I should stop then." Helios smirks, pulling out of me.

I glare at him, biting the inside of my cheek to stop from begging him.

He growls, "You want me back?"

I cross my arms, unwilling to bend.

Helios reaches down, pressing his thumb to my clit, and I can't stop my eyes from rolling in pleasure. "My poor kitten. So empty." He pours heat into his thumb, singeing my clit, and I lift my hips greedily.

"You need me to fill you?" Helios asks, withdrawing his fingers.

I bristle, pushing him away and sitting up. "Don't bother."

He grabs me, shoving me down and pulling my wrists above my head. "My sassy hellcat."

I growl, glaring up at him.

Helios thrusts inside me, and I cry out, opening my thighs wide for him. I pull at his hold on my wrists, not to get free but to give the illusion that's what I want.

Helios pulls out of me again, and my cunt throbs in needy frustration. "Do you need me?"

I look up at him, clenching my fists.

"Do you?" he demands.

There's something in the way his eyes gleam that makes me think this isn't a game. He isn't trying to manipulate me. He needs to hear this from me.

"You know I do," I snarl, still glaring.

He thrusts back inside me. "That's all I needed to hear." His lips pull into that maddening smirk that sets my blood alight.

"You smug fucker," I moan as he starts to fuck me, his cock stretching my pussy deliciously.

Helios slams his lips to mine. "That's right. Because I know how much you love being full of me."

I deepen the kiss, snarling into his mouth, "Asshole."

Helios hisses. "You're tightening on this asshole's cock."

"Fuck. I hate you so much!" I cry out.

"Come for me," Helios commands. "Come for the man you claim to hate."

My body arches, and I scream his name, coming hard. My whole body trembles with the ecstasy of my release. Helios kisses me hard, muffling his own roar of pleasure as he spills inside me, filling me. I bite his tongue, and his answering growl sends a shiver down my spine. My pussy flutters and clenches around him again as he rolls us, pulling me with him to sprawl on top of him.

He kisses my temple, slick with sweat. "I love you."

I mumble incoherently, looking up at him.

He raises a blond brow. "What was that?"

I mumble again, only fractionally louder.

"Sorry. I missed it again." He turns his head, hovering his ear in front of my lips.

"Love you," I grumble, still quietly.

Helios's smile is bright enough to fill the galaxy as he looks up at me. "You're obsessed with me." I groan and roll off him, but he pulls me back on top of him, nuzzling into my neck. "Have you told demon daddy I'm staying here?"

I shake my head.

"Are you going to?"

I shrug. "Hades probably wouldn't hear it. He's so lost."

Helios tucks a lock of black hair behind my ear. "I know it's been awful seeing them both like this."

I exhale heavily. "He's insufferable without P."

"He is. But I know how much she means to you."

"She's my best friend."

Helios nuzzles his nose with mine. "You've been texting her."

I frown. "How do you know?"

"I didn't until now," he replies, smiling softly. "We'll get her back, kitten."

I nod, and as I nuzzle closer against his warmth, I realize

how quiet my head is at this moment—just him and me. Bliss.[15]

---

15   The Queen & The King Chapter 43

THE GREENHOUSE ON OLYMPUS IS A PLANT PARADISE. All available space is bursting with life, thriving greenery, and color. It's so at odds with the other perfectly plotted crops right outside. I suppose this is the one place where Persephone can show the slightest bit of individuality. Though I suspect Persephone had just created this haven since regaining her memory. It's a slight rebellion from her. She's curling a vine around her hand when I knock on the paned glass.

Her head snaps up, her eyes going wide when she sees me. She runs to me, and I see the face of my friend. My true friend. Her eyes have lost that alarming sheen of naivete, and instead, a familiar cunning has taken its place. This is the Persephone I remember, the one you underestimate at your own peril, whose pretty petals hide just as pretty thorns.

"So you do remember."

She pulls me into a hug, the comforting scent of roses wafting over me. Wrapping my arms around her, I squeeze her tightly, lifting her off her feet. She needs someone who knows her, the real her, right now.

She grins as she looks down at me. "How are you?"

That is such a loaded question. I'm practically staring down another of Zeus's bolts. I put her back on her feet. "Well, I'm living in the Underworld because your brother-in-law wants to kill me, so…"

She tilts her head, some of that red flashing in her hair as it moves. "Because of the war?"

The war. Fucking hate that word now. Fuck war. Fuck

choosing sides. "I haven't… said which side I'll fight for."

I'm starting to resent the implication that I have to fight. Sometimes, a warrior never wants to go back to battle. Sometimes, I wish I didn't know the many ways to hold a sword or how many ways blood can drip from the edge of a blade.

Persephone's eyes search mine, and I have to stop myself from stepping back from the way her sun-marked eyes peer into me. I may have sway over the sun, but Persephone contains all the power in her eyes. Nothing can hide from her.

"How's Mellie?" she probes, even as she moves back to the table of seedlings. She feigns like she's looking away, but I know she's aware of my every movement. Sometimes, it feels like her vines are wrapped around my mind, listening to my thoughts.

Fingering one of the bright petals, I muse, "She… brought me to the Underworld to protect me." Our bed. She brought me to a place she despised, a place she swore never to stay in again. For me. To keep me safe. My glow brightens more just thinking about it. I doubt my glow will dim for years after that. "She's kind of obsessed with me."

Persephone laughs, even as she digs her fingers into the soil of the smaller pots, the earth looking for her, reaching for her.

"I brought you a present." I smirk, pulling her new cell phone from my pocket. Despite searching for the old cell phone, none of the ghosts could locate it in the Underworld. I have not had the heart to tell Melinoë about it. I know how much it means to her to think that Persephone will one day read the messages she had sent during this time.

She takes the phone from me, her lips twitching when she sees there is only one contact saved in it.

I shake my head. "For emergencies only. I doubt you'd be able to charge it without her catching on."

"I'm surprised you got away with not giving Mellie the new number." She smiles, tucking the phone into her sedate gown.

I can't help but smile back. Despite everything, I'm lighter than ever before. "She doesn't know I'm here. She texts you, you know."

I'm going to find that fucking phone.

Persephone focuses on the flowers again. "I miss my crazy best friend."

"She's missing you too." I pause. "Hades is… not doing

well without you, petal."

She tenses, her lips flattening, and for a moment, the air in the greenhouse becomes oppressive with power. Heady power. My head spins a little from being subjected to it, but before I can ask her to dial it back, Demeter's voice calls from the house, summoning Persephone back in, and it vanishes.

"I know," she adds, wiping her hands on her dress before pressing a kiss to my cheek. "Will you gather everyone tonight, and I'll call in?"

I nod. "Seven. New York time."

Demeter calls, "Persephone!"

Persephone's eyes flash with rage and that oppressive power returns. Her jaw clenches and I swear that when the sunlight hits her hair, the usual red in the brown strands looks black as pitch. She takes a deep breath, regaining control over it again, and squeezes my arm. "Look after them, Helios."

"I will." Persephone smiles as she leaves me alone in the greenhouse.

Chapter Thirty-Eight
Melinoë

I STRETCH IN BED, REACHING FOR THE WARM BODY I FELL ASLEEP WITH, but my hand only meets cool sheets. My brows furrow, awareness of the danger he's in flooding my consciousness. My eyelids fly open, and I look at his side of the bed. The sheets are rumpled but cool. He's been gone for at least an hour. I climb out of bed, stumbling through to the bathroom.

"Helios?"

My heart sinks when I find it empty. Shit, shit, shit. But he's safe here. Right? Hades wouldn't let Zeus take him from his realm… Unless… No. He wouldn't.

I start to get dressed, ready to search the palace for him, the whole realm, if I need to. He promised he wouldn't leave. As I'm tying my laces, a bright flash fills the room. When it dims enough, I see Helios standing in my room, his posture uncensored, arrogant, and unharmed.

I narrow my eyes at his back, gritting my teeth though the relief I feel is palpable. "Where were you?"

Helios spins, his stupid skin glowing. "Hi! You were sleeping—"

"Where. Were. You?" I grit out, my body coiled with anger.

Helios blinks. "Olympus."

My heart stutters with panic as I try to decide how to feel about Helios going straight into the belly of the beast. While Olympus is the most dangerous place he could have gone, he probably went to see Persephone. An internal war rages as I try to decide whether to stab him or kiss him.

"You… saw Persephone?" I ask, my body relaxing slightly.

Helios nods and kneels in front of me. "I managed to get her a phone. She had asked Hades to get one to her."

I tip my head in confusion. How had she spoken with Hades? I hadn't dreamwalked him. Since Morphie couldn't even locate her dream, we'd given up on even trying.

Helios strokes my cheek, reading my silent questions. "She remembers, Mel."

My eyes go wide, my jaw dropping.

"I don't know how it happened, but she was in Hades' dream last night, and she remembers everything. Hades came to me early this morning to ask me to take her a cell phone."

She went to his dream without a dreamwalker? The mating bond must be in play now that her memory is back. It is the only way they could see one another, and with the bond pulled so taut for so long…

I shake my head, snapping myself from my thoughts. "She has her phone?" I jump up, scrambling for my phone.

Helios stands and watches me with a pained expression. "We couldn't find her old phone, Mellie. She has a new one."

My heart sinks a little, but it's better than nothing. "What's her number?"

Helios walks over to me, cupping my cheeks again. "For emergencies only, kitten."

I blink. "But what if you're being a weirdo stalker, and I have to tell her?"

He laughs, kissing me softly. "But that's not an emergency, is it?" I give him a look that tells him I beg to differ. "We'll have a group call with her tonight," he says.

I squeal, smiling brightly. "Okay, good! I hope Hades doesn't come. He'll hog all of her attention and bore her to death."

Helios smiles. "He has to be present. He's the only one with her new number."

"But he'll spend all the time being a big mush ball and kissy facing her," I protest, grimacing.

Helios presses kisses along my cheek. "I know. It's awful."

I sigh dramatically and fall back on the bed. Helios laughs, watching me.

"Why are you being so silly?" he asks, a new kind of affection in his voice.

I press the back of my hand against my forehead, sighing dramatically. "I want to hang out with my best friend without stupid boys."

Helios climbs on top of me, kissing me softly. "You don't want any stupid boys around?"

I wrap myself around him. "I guess you can stay for a while…"

Helios smothers my face in kisses. "How kind of you, my Goddess of Nightmares."

I snag his lips with mine, kissing him deeply. Helios rolls us so I'm on top, and I growl into his lips, pinning his arms down. "I don't like waking up alone." I rock my hips against him, teasing him and biting back a moan when I feel how hard he already is.

"Is that right?" Helios's question is a deep moan.

I kiss down his neck, nipping at the sensitive skin.

"Were you cold, baby?"

I growl. "No."

"Not at all?"

I suck on his neck. "I wasn't cold. I was horny." My lips hover over his, and when Helios lifts to press his lips against mine, I pull back, teasing him. He snaps his teeth at me, growling.

"But you weren't here," I croon.

Helios rolls us again so I'm beneath him, and he grinds his cock against me. "I'm here now."

"You are."

Helios smirks and burns our clothes away before burying himself inside me, claiming my body. We come together in a tangle of limbs, moans and whispered curses filling the air. He fucks me with abandon until we're both close to the agonizing bliss of release. Helios looks down at me, panting, his eyes black with need.

"You want to hear those words, sunboy? The words you crave from me? Then fuck me harder."

Helios obeys, his hips slamming into me so hard that my teeth chatter from the force.

"I love you, Helios!" I scream, coming so hard that my vision blurs.

He groans, digging his fingers into my hip. "Say it again. Please."

"I love you. Fuck…" The words slip from my lips as easy as breathing. My orgasm feels like it shatters my soul, or is it this horrific and glorious emotion?

"Again," Helios grates out. I can feel him holding back his orgasm, his body rippling with it.

I meet his eyes, my body soft and welcoming beneath his. My pussy clenches around his cock, begging for his release. "I love you," I say, and even I can hear the change in my voice, the truth of my words.

Helios roars, the chandelier shaking from the force of it. Sweat drips down the side of his face, and I lick it from his jaw as he fills me with his cum. He kisses me deeply, moaning against my lips, his body heavy on mine. I curl around him, keeping him locked to me. He brushes the hair back from my face, his lips pulled into that maddening smug smile.

"Look how smug you are." I roll my eyes but can't stop myself from returning his smile.

Helios laughs, kissing me again. We stay in bed, tangled in one another, until it's time for the call with P.[16]

THE ONLY WARNING I GET IS THE RISE OF THE HAIR ON THE BACK OF MY NECK. Then the world rocks and the ground trembles beneath me. I am the only one to sense it, to understand it. It's the shifting of ancient, Primordial power. A power that is a part of mine. A celestial power. The power of Gaia is free again. Which means…

"Melinoë!" I shout. Storming through the palace, I start off at a walk but soon escalate into a frantic run. I am the only celestial god in the Underworld at the moment. Well, besides Nyx, but she is bound to non-interference. The ground trembles for me, sending me hard into the wall. The ghosts watch me. They are confused, sensing nothing wrong with the cosmic order.

I straighten and sprint to the kitchen. Melinoë is there with Cerberus, who looks just as on edge as I feel. Closing the distance, I struggle to remain upright as Gaia's power unwinds the celestial order. "Baby. I have to go."

She straightens, grabbing my cheeks, her eyes flashing with concern. "Go? No. You promised."

Fuck, I don't have time even to explain why I have to go.

"I have to go," I repeat, jerking as the change in power affects the sun. Melinoë feels it with her fingers, but she won't bend.

"You promised."

I know I should keep that promise. I press my lips hard against hers, and she softens so perfectly against me. "I will be back."

She stiffens in my arms and shoves me back. Melinoë glares at me, her expression ripping my heart from my chest. This is how she looked at me before we came to the Underworld, before she whispered her love for me.

"Fine. Leave." She spins on her heel, walking away from me.

I don't have time to explain, and I know she won't listen to me right now. Fuck.

I flash from the Underworld to my sisters, prepared to finally pick a side, no matter what comes next. Selene is trying to steady herself against the wall, and Eos is crouched on the floor, both suffering the same effects as I.

"Gaia," I whisper, knowing they'll understand without words.

Selene nods, pale from the power shift. "What do we do?"

I grimace as my stomach roils. Will she ever forgive me for this? "We summon our allies, and we fight like hell."[17]

Chapter Forty
Melinoë

H E LEFT. HE FUCKING LEFT. After he swore to me that he wouldn't.

Fury churns within me, fury and something else. A foreign emotion that I don't want to look at too closely. My heart feels as though it's being grated with every breath, my lungs burning as I draw in oxygen I don't even fucking want. Even the voices in my head are deathly silent. Alone. I am truly alone. Even Cerberus left soon after Helios, his heads snapping toward the kitchen door before he barrelled out.

I'm still standing in the place I was when he fucking betrayed me. My legs feel like lead, superglued to this space. This is the space where my heart was ripped from my chest and trampled so thoroughly that there is no saving it. Helios is gone. He broke his promise to me and fled.

I don't know how long I stand there, numb but aching, before I feel the ground shake beneath me. Not in the way it did before he left. This is not a power shift but a physical one. My legs are moving before I plan for it. I head toward the kitchen window, but I don't make it that far. A bellow splits the air, and I collapse to the ground with my hands pressed over my ears. Pain pierces my head, my eardrums rupturing from the frequency and volume of that roar. I manage to get to my feet, dread sitting heavily on me as I approach the window.

Fuck, fuck, fuck.

My fingers grip the sink, and my eyes widen as I watch Typhon wreak havoc across the plane. Once again, I am frozen, though not in the same way as before. This is fear. True fear. It's an emotion I didn't know I was capable of.

The fear becomes terror when I see Hades charge toward him, riding on Cerberus's back.

"What the fuck are you doing, Hades?"

I watch uselessly as Hades throws his bident at the beast, the blade piercing him, and then I gape in horror as other creatures are born from his blood.

Fuck, I've got to do something.

Forcing my feet to move, I sprint to my room and pull on my battle leathers. They are still encrusted with blood from the last time I used them. I smile wickedly at the memory but push it aside when Typhon roars again.

We need more people. Hades and I will be no match for a beast of his size and power. I run to my window and breathe a sigh of relief when I see Zeus and Poseidon have arrived. And is that…

I gasp when I see a flash of white wings collide with Hades, saving him from being trampled. A gold spike thrusts from the ground in his place.

Persephone looks down at Hades with such love, and the way she kisses him… She's back. She's home.

I look around, thinking. We still need more troops. My decision made, I shadow away.

I pay another unwanted visit to Apollo. He is so keen to get me out of his presence that he sends out a blast to everyone he can think of without me having to do much threatening.

Ares is the first to respond. The God of War is always itching for a fight. We formulate a plan within minutes and are on the battlefield.

Persephone blinks at me, confused, and I watch as she slowly takes in my filthy leathers, relief shining in her sky-blue eyes.

"What? You thought you'd take on these cretins without me?" She just continues to stare at me, so I add, "It doesn't make sense to clean the leathers. The blood makes me look even more terrifying."

She pulls me into her, wrapping her arms around me. Her rose scent mixes with the foul stench of fresh Titan blood, and I wrinkle my nose. "I missed you, Mel."

I pull back after a moment, the Titans growling and snarling impatiently from behind the force field. "I brought reinforcements."

Ares takes control, and with a battle cry, I launch myself into their front lines, reveling in the feeling of muscle, sinew, and bones giving way beneath my blade. My trusty bat is strapped to my back for when their numbers dwindle, and I can have real fun.

In the back of my mind, I think of Helios. What if he fights against us? Will I be able to bring myself to kill him if it comes down to it? What if he harms Hades, Persephone, or Berry?

The thought makes me see red, and while I've never felt farther from insanity, I allow myself to lean into the instincts that come to the surface when I have plummeted. The brutal, violent, animalistic side of me comes into play as I fight to defend my queen, my king, and my realm.

The battle rages on, and I make sure to always keep one eye on my best friend, though she is a skilled fighter and appears more than able to handle herself.

I feel a ripple in the Underworld, a shift of power, and I whirl toward it. Hades stands with his back to me, his shoulders tense as he stares into the distance. I shadow to Hades and feel the whimper escape more than hear it. My gaze lands on the Titan of the Sun, standing with his own army.

Helios's honey-golden gaze locks with mine, his lips pulling into a crooked smile. He winks at Hades before turning and unleashing his power on the Titans.

I release a breath I didn't know I was holding, and another tear rolls down my cheek.[18]

Chapter Forty-One

Helios

WEARING ARMOR AGAIN FELT A LITTLE TOO FAMILIAR and comfortable like I am still nothing more than a cog in a massive machine of war. I am just that boy again, nothing more than a son begging his parents to find him worthy enough to come first in their lives.

"Are you sure about your choice?" Eos's soft voice snaps my eyes up. She is similarly dressed in sunset battle leathers, but her eyes are still gentle and kind.

I nod. "There's no going back now."

"You sure she's worth it?" Selene sneers, her armor shining silver to my gold.

"She is."

Selene rolls her eyes. "Whatever. Can we go?"

I pull the ties of my forearm braces, shaking my head. "We're still waiting on a couple more people."

Eos blinks. "People? What have you done, Helios?"

The knock on the door stops me from explaining, and I swing the door open, already knowing who's on the other side. Prometheus nods at me solemnly, holding out his arm for me to clasp in a shake. The guy might be the God of Forethought, but he was stuck in the customs of the past. I clasp his arm, nodding in acknowledgment. "Any issues with the recruits?"

"Recruits?" Selene parrots, trying to figure out what's going on.

Prometheus shakes his head. "No, they're all ready for you."

I release his arm, moving out of the way so the other Titan can step in. "Perfect." I pause for a second before facing my confused sisters. "Prometheus has been helping me get some things in place in case this happened." Eos looks at the other Titan, trying to figure out what I was saying. "I knew whichever side we chose, we needed to make sure we won. So I decided to weigh the odds in our favor."

Prometheus covers one hand over the other in front of him. "I know what it's like to make the unpopular choice and to turn against family."

Prometheus and his brother, Iapetus, Titan of Afterthought, were the only Titans to side with the Olympians against his father and older brother in the first Titan War. When your older brother is the strongest of Titans, you have to choose carefully.

I can fucking relate.

"Wait, don't you know who's going to win?" Selene sniffs, looking Prometheus over scathingly. "Isn't that how you turned on us last time?"

His eyes flash for a second before his formal facade returns. "Much like your mother," Selene flinches at that, "I can only predict to a certain percentage of certainty, and that percentage is not one hundred percent."

Eos's eyes widened slightly. Our mother's sight isn't perfect either. The future is ever-changing and fluid. Prometheus's powers must be similar, but that is not a well-known fact. It is, in fact, a closely guarded secret. Prometheus just revealed a great vulnerability to us.

Selene locks eyes with me, her silver eyes clashing with my gold ones. Understanding flickers there, and without words, I know I can count on her in the coming battle. I hold out my hand to my sisters, and they slowly take it. In a flash, I take us all into the Underworld, depositing us directly into the middle of chaos.

The Olympians all tense as we reappear. There's an audible inhale of air, everyone waiting to see what we'll do next. I scan the battle, looking for Melinoë. I know she will be here. My eyes connect with Hades first.

I keep my gaze on him as I flash more Titans to the battlefield, Titans who are just like me. They don't want to just mindlessly follow their kind. They hate Kronos and remember what it was like under his rule. These are the tricksters and Titans of lesser power who suffered under the past.

Hades's sapphire eyes flash at me, waiting. Like everyone else, he is expecting betrayal. I wave at him, smirking as other gods appear. A strangled sound draws my attention, and I see the love of my life in bloodstained leathers.

Her eyes are vulnerable, her emotions flickering between them, and my lips twitch.

She's furious with me. She has a right to be. I know I broke my promise, and I know it is the only promise she has ever asked of me, probably from anyone ever. It will take some work to get her to open up to me like that again, but we'll have eternity. No matter how many times she shuts the door in my face, I'll just find a new way to pick the lock. She can run, but there's nowhere I won't follow. I will always find her.

I drink her in before shooting a wink at Hades and turning to lead my sisters and the other gods into the fray. Selene nods at me and takes off with her two silver daggers. She slips and slides along the soaked ground, going under legs and slashing tendons. Eos swings her sword, knocking a Titan in the jaw before she headbutts them. I know better than to worry about them right now. No, right now, I have a score to settle.

Even as I close the distance, more sunlight flashes into the Underworld. The gods Prometheus had recruited, riding my invitation down to the battle. Astraeus, Titan of the Stars and Eos's husband, lands in a sparkle of starlight, saluting me as he launches into the fray. In another flash of sunlight, Themis, Titaness of Divine Law and Order, appears, her eyes bound in the typical white blindfold.

I keep running. Even as the other gods arrive, the ones who are older than Titans, stuck in the generation between the Primordials and the Titans, more commonly referred to as Primes. Unlike their parents, they are not bound by the treaty of the First Gods to non-interference. Hekate and Thanatos greet their siblings as they arrive, both already battered from the conflict. As Typhon moved across the Underworld, monsters spawned from his blood, attacking anything in their path. The Giants had been released and are fighting the Olympians, no doubt remembering their unsolved issues from the Gigantomachy.

But they were not my target.

My lips twitch when I see him. Today seems to be the day for father-son reunions and ass-kickings. He sees me closing in and stretches his hands out on either side before slamming his palms together, sending a piercing beam of light toward me. Ducking, I wince as the ray hits me in the shoulder, cutting through my arm, skin, muscle, and bone. Fuck, I forgot how much that laser shit hurts.

I may be sunlight, but my father is all light, and I am already at a disadvantage with Apollo on the field of battle.

Love that little side effect of giving over a bit of my control to him all those years ago. Selene will be feeling the effects, too. Where Apollo went, Artemis almost always followed.

My sunlight flares, and I focus it on my father, our powers clashing in a single beam, power against power. I grit my teeth. With sheer force of will, I take a step forward, then another. Yeah, he's way more powerful than me, infinitely more, but I have the motivation he doesn't. I am fighting for the people I care for.

One step.

Persephone's laugh turns to a snort.

Another step.

Eos's shy smile.

Another.

Selene's face when she's surprised.

One more step.

Melinoë.

I close the distance, not caring that I have several holes in my body from his power. They are already healing. I grab my father's hands and yank them to the sides before plowing my fist into his face. The adamantium knuckles on my fingers slice through his skin and break his jaw. He screams, and it plays like music in my ears. Melinoë would love this. My next punch sends him flying, and I laugh as I close the distance, watching him try to crawl away. Normally, I would be shocked to have been able to bring my father so low, but at the moment, I don't really give a fuck.

He's one more thing in the way of Melinoë riding me off into the sunset with me, and that is a very bad place to be. I stare down at his crumpled, pathetic body, and without looking at her, I speak to my mother before she can drive her weapon into my back.

"Run. While you can," I say, my body healing from the wounds my father had inflicted on me. "Take him and run, but you better hope Hades can't find you. This is the last thing I will ever do for you. We are no longer family."

My mother drops her sword and hurries around me to my injured father.

"Run," I repeat. "Don't ever come back."

She shoots me a look of regret twined with anger before vanishing with my father.

I'm free of their bullshit. The last thread of familiar connection between us has been cut. Now, it is time to find my little hellcat and start a future with meaning. A future full of chaos, insanity, and significance. My eyes sweep the battlefield, unsurprised to see that my side is now winning.

The Titans have been forced into cells after being trounced, and Typhon is defeated. I don't see Kronos, so I am sure he has been taken care of, too.

Where is she?[19]

Chapter Forty-Two
Melinoë

THE AIR IS THICK WITH DEATH AND RAGE. I trudge through the slowly rebuilding prison, dragging my bat along the bars of the cells. Mangled Titans are slowly knitting back together within. The only sounds are groans of pain as they slowly heal and the clang of my wooden bat against the metal. There are far fewer now. Some were launched into the void, lost forever. We should have sent them all into that pit of unending suffering, but Hades had made it clear that the void was to remain closed. The threat would be too great for everyone on the battlefield while they were open.

I zero in on a Titan who took a chunk out of my arm in the fight, and I approach his cell, wrapping my hand around the bar as I peer in. He hisses at me, trying to lunge for me, but he is still missing one of his legs and both of his arms. It will take a while for those to grow back.

I grin at him and push away from the cell, continuing my patrol and ensuring everyone is locked up tightly. I have lived in the Underworld for millennia, and not once in my memory have the cells been breached... until now. Hades and Persephone will take time to come up with a way to ensure this doesn't happen again, but the risk is still there until they recapture the one who continues to evade them.

Kronos was on the battlefield. I saw him far in the distance, watching on as his minions did his bidding.

Coward.

My boots squelch as I walk through puddles of blood and guts, probably some excrement, but I don't care. We fucking won.

One of the Titans charges to the front of his cell, and I hiss at him as he collides with the iron bars, reaching for me. I slam my bat into his hand, and he wails in pain, his fingers bending in gruesome angles.

"Melinoë?" Helios's frantic voice cuts through my thoughts, through the snarls and groans of the prisoners, and I whirl toward him. My gaze immediately finds him. His light-colored leathers are now caked in blood and mud, his perfect face marred with cuts, bruises, and the grime of battle. Even his usually perfect hair is matted, windswept, and flecked with Titan blood, the blood of his people, probably his family.

"Baby," Helios says, calmer this time, but he doesn't move toward me. He can obviously see the fury in my eyes.

Am I grateful that he fought with us? That he survived? Of course I am. But he still broke his promise to me. He still left.

Helios takes a tentative step toward me, and I glare at him, but my heart thunders in my chest, my skin tingling in anticipation of his touch.

He stops just in front of me. "Hi," he breathes.

"You left," I grate out, trying to keep my voice even. "You broke your promise."

"Traitorous filth," a Titan sneers, and I slam my bat into the metal again, making the bars reverberate.

Helios seems to pay no attention to the Titan as he grabs me, wrapping his arms around my waist. In a flash, we're in our bedroom in the palace. "Kitten."

I shove him, growling, unable to get a handle on any of the confusing emotions flooding through me. "You fucking left! What if Zeus had found you? Captured you? Killed you?" I snarl.

Helios grabs my hand, pulling me back against him. He slams his lips to mine, and I struggle in his arms, shoving at his chest. He continues to hold me, to kiss me, and when his tongue slides along the seam of my lips, when I get that first intoxicating taste of him, I begin to melt, as usual.

He pulls back when I stop struggling, his intense gaze pinning me. "I didn't have time to explain."

I growl, my jaw clenched.

"I chose a side," he begins but pauses to kiss me again. "The second you chose to keep me safe. The second you…" He pauses, considering his words. "The second you chose me."

"And now I'm fucking changing my decision. Fucking

idiot," I growl, though I make no move to get away from him. His warmth seeps through our filthy leathers and into my skin, into my soul.

Helios's lips twitch, and he kisses me again. "Liar."

I start to kiss him back when another wave of anger surges through me. He put himself in danger. He made me think he had chosen to fight for the enemy. I slap him hard across his face, the sound filling the room.

Helios's answering groan stokes the flame in my core, the fire that only burns for him.

"There wasn't time to explain," he says, his eyes nearly black as he looks down at me.

My fists clench, and I growl, grabbing his face roughly. "If you ever leave me like that again, I'll slowly kill you and mail each of your sisters a collection of your body parts. Then I will put the remains in the river Styx."

Helios moans low. "Fuck, you're so hot. You know that, right?"

"Shut the fuck up." I slam my lips to his, tangling my fingers in his knotted hair and pressing my body close. The fear of losing the other emanates from us both, and Helios lifts me easily, kissing me wildly as he walks toward the bathroom. I groan as he slams me against the shower wall, clumsily turning the dial. The water is freezing for a split second before Helios blindly reaches for the temperature dial, turning it so the water is near scalding.

The sound of the spray muffles our moans only slightly as we tear at each other's leathers, desperate to be skin on skin. The armor and leather litter the bathroom as we chuck it aimlessly away, only breaking our kiss for the briefest of moments when absolutely necessary.

Helios pulls back when we're fully naked, his heavy length pressing against my core.

"I am always on your side," he says breathlessly.

"You fucking better be, asshole," I growl, tightening my fingers in his hair.

Helios smiles wolfishly. "I love you."

I moan as his cock presses teasingly against my entrance. "Don't care."

Helios growls into my ear, "Liar."

He forges into me with a quick, brutal thrust. My core tightens at the feeling of him filling me, his cock stretching my cunt so perfectly.

I cry out, arching my back off the wall. "I'm so fucking angry with you."

Helios drags his lips over my cheek, back to my lips, and

thrusts harder inside me. "Liar."

"Hate you…" I moan, my toes curling in pleasure.

Helios digs his fingers into my ass as he fucks me frantically. "Liar, liar, liar."

"Need you," I grate out, arching more into him, dragging my nails down his arms.

"Say it," Helios growls into my lips, his nails digging into my ass cheeks as his hips slam into me.

"I-l–" I cry out, "love you."

"Yes, you fucking do." He bites my lip hard, pushing me over the edge and into pleasure, my orgasm coming with a scream.

Helios follows me, his own admission of feelings wrapping around my heart and sealing it back together.[20]

---

20   The Queen & The King Chapters 60 - 69

EPILOGUE
MELINOË &HELIOS

I WANDER THROUGH THE PALACE HALLS, toward the kitchen for a much-needed midnight snack. The marble is cold against my bare feet. Every morning when I wake up, a brand new pair of slippers is positioned at my side of the bed, the prime position for me to shove my feet into, but I always kick them away. The palace is anticipating my needs like a mother hen, but I enjoy the bite of the cold against the soles of my feet. I pad down the darkened halls and slip into the kitchen. It's weird being here without Hades or Persephone.

Helios and I have been looking after Cerberus while the lovebirds are on their honeymoon, and it hasn't been complete torture. I enjoy spending time with Berry, and even though I can tell he's missing his mom and dad, the depression has lifted. He knows they're coming back and that they're safe.

Helios has been annoying as usual, but it's been… nice having him here the past ten days. He helps alleviate some of the unease I feel being here, and though my scars still ache dully, he always seems to be able to tell and casually places a warm hand on the small of my back or my thigh.

Mushy dickhead.

The voices are still present, but I seem to be more in control of them. I've been working on it. Visualizing a dial with the ability to turn them down if need be. The insanity still dances at the edges of my psyche, but there's something comforting about it now. Maybe because I know that if I do plummet, I have people who will be there with me to pull me back into myself.

I open the fridge, the light illuminating the kitchen, and start to sample from various boxes.

"You left."

I peer around the door of the fridge, sucking on a spoon.

Helios is standing in the doorway of the kitchen, looking so perfectly sex rumpled. His sweatpants hang low on his hips, washboard abs on display for my entertainment. I slowly pull the spoon from my lips, my eyes roaming over him.

"I didn't realize I was in your custody," I say, my gaze challenging.

Helios pushes off the doorframe. "It's not fair."

I quirk a brow, tracking his movements as he prowls closer. "What?"

"How much better that shirt looks on you."

I look down at the shirt that hangs loosely on me. It's just a simple long-sleeved beige jersey T-shirt, but I love the way his clothes dwarf me.

"I didn't want to blind Thanatos if I stumbled upon him."

Helios laughs, wrapping his arms around my waist and pulling me into him. "I missed you."

I roll my eyes. "I left the bed less than five minutes ago."

"But I came back from the bathroom, and you were gone," he whines dramatically, nuzzling my hair.

"So dramatic." I roll my eyes. "And clingy. And annoying."

Helios smiles into my hair. "You fucking love it."

"I'm about to show you how much I love piercing your skin with a blade," I growl.

Helios groans, brushing his lips over my temple. "Fuck, you are so perfect, always tempting me with a good time." Helios cups my ass and lifts me onto the kitchen island, nestling his hips between my legs. "My perfect girlfriend."

I tunnel my fingers in his hair, about to, not so politely, remind him I am, in fact, not his girlfriend, but he pulls back, an eyebrow raised, waiting.

Fuck. The bet.

Three days ago, Helios challenged me to a knife-throwing contest. At the last second, he distracted me, and I lost because I threw my last blade at his stupid face, just missing him by half an inch. If I had won, Helios would have had to admit to every single person we met for the next three months that he was stalking me and didn't know how to satisfy a woman. If he won, I wasn't allowed to say that I wasn't his girlfriend.

The penalty for that was… grave. If I said it, we would live together for three months. I force my mouth closed and glare at him.

He laughs and kisses me. "I'll get you living with me yet, kitten," Helios murmurs into my mouth.

I smile against his lips, allowing myself to bask in him. To love him. To be content. To be happy. To be me.

Helios

I CHEATED. I already bought a place for us in New York. Her place isn't right for us, and I know my place isn't either. So I bought a new place, an entire townhouse in Manhattan. I already have a crew working on it, turning it into the perfect creepy crawly house for us. By the time I am done, she will never want to leave. It starts at three months, but before she knows it, our lives will be completely intertwined, and she'll never want to leave. I've already planned out the first fifteen proposals, and I know how she'll say no each time, but it won't matter because I'll still ask.

Even as we stay in the Underworld watching over the monstrous dog that I suspect has been eating the ass portion of my pants when I'm not looking, my body hums with contentment. A near-constant glow lingers on my skin.

"I have a present for you," I murmur to her as I pull back and look down at her in the glow of the still-open fridge.

She glances up at me, her eyes shimmering with avarice. "Give now."

"Say, please."

She growls, grabbing my cock and squeezing hard. I wheeze out a breath, the pained sound followed by a groan. I quickly hold up the box. She snatches it from me, releasing my cock a moment later.

"This better not be a ring," she warns.

I cough, feeling the blood rushing back to my cock. "It's not, open it."

She flips open the jewelry box, frowning at the single earring. My lips twitch. "I had an opportunity to speak to Hekate while we've been here." I take the earring out and put it in one of Melinoë's ears. "For when you get lost, you'll be able to find me, and I'll always be able to find you."

I turn my head to show her my matching earring, the only one in that ear. She reaches out to touch the piercings.

"So, I'll always know where you are?"

There's the slightest hesitation in her voice, as if she's scared that she's misunderstood.

I smirk, kissing her head. "Not always. Hekate spelled it to be triggered for when you get lost in your head. I know how obsessed you are with being chased. If I knew where you were all the time, it would take all the fun out of things."

She hits me in the stomach at that but reaches up to rub her piercing, and in that silence, I hear her words from the time she got lost in her head. Helios. Safe.

I'll be your safety, Melinoë, and if I can't pull you back from your madness, I'll dive deep into it with you. I lift her chin, kissing her softly.

"I love you," I whisper into her lips.

I don't need her to say it back. I can bask in the knowledge that she loves me and all the ways she shows me.

"I love you too," she answers, making my heart pound. "Or whatever."

It's perfect for now. At least until she's got the ring I bought last week around her finger, but I'm a patient guy in love with an absolutely perfectly insane girl.

She might think of herself as a nightmare, but she'll always be my dream.[21]

The Love & Fate Series will continue with...

Dionysus

&

Ariadne